MOUNTAIN MELODY

They were sisters, Cherry and Loyce, but as different as day and night. Cherry was vivacious and outgoing, with everything in life before her. Loyce was quiet and withdrawn, still bearing the scars of her fiancé's untimely death. But at Crossways, their grandfather's delightful hunting lodge in the Blue Ridge Mountains, they find themselves drawn together — in complicity. The reason is Jonathan Gayle, a handsome lawyer who unwittingly leads them into a strange romantic triangle.

Books by Peggy Gaddis
in the Linford Romance Library:

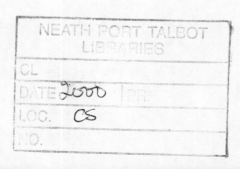

PEGGY GADDIS

◆

MOUNTAIN MELODY

Complete and Unabridged

LINFORD
Leicester

First published in the
United States of America

First Linford Edition
published December 1995

British Library CIP Data

Gaddis, Peggy
    Mountain melody.—Large print ed.—
Linford romance library
I. Title II. Series
813.52 [F]

    ISBN 0–7089–7793–6

Published by
F. A. Thorpe (Publishing) Ltd.
Anstey, Leicestershire
Set by Words & Graphics Ltd.
Anstey, Leicestershire
Printed and bound in Great Britain by
T. J. Press (Padstow) Ltd., Padstow, Cornwall

This book is printed on acid-free paper

1

CHERRY BRAMBLETT stood on the station platform with a pleasant smile pinned to her young face as the two portly, middle-aged men clambered aboard the train, laden with their fishing paraphernalia, leaving Crossways Lodge reluctantly after a weekend crammed to the final hour with pleasure.

The train pulled out with the two men still on the steps, waving, calling assurances that they would return very soon. When at last they had gone, Cherry turned away and drew a deep breath of relief.

As she moved toward the waiting car to return to the lodge, the station agent called to her and came out from the office:

"Wait a minute, Miss Cherry."

"Oh, hello, Tom. How are Grace

and the children?" Cherry smiled at him.

The raw-boned man revealed discolored teeth.

"The boy's pindlin', Miss Cherry, but I reckon he'll be fine soon's schools out," he answered, and jerked a thumb over his shoulder toward the waiting room. "Fellow here come down on the train says he wants to go to Crossways. I told him I'd see would you take him."

The man had emerged from the waiting room now and was coming toward them with swift strides. He was well above medium height, and he had an air of anxiety that puzzled Cherry.

"Miss Bramblett, this here fellow says he's Jonathan Gayle, from up Chicago way," Tom presented the man, and walked away with the air of one who had done his duty and now washed his hands of the whole business.

"I understand you operate Crossways Lodge, Miss Bramblett," said Jonathan

2

Gayle. "I'd like to spend a few weeks there on vacation."

Cherry looked him over with a swift appraisal that took note of his pleasantly unobtrusive good looks, his dark hair, his troubled eyes.

"I'm sorry, Mr. Gayle, but we only accept guests with previous reservations who have been carefully screened as to references," Cherry told him quietly, making no effort to soften the baldness of her words. "And you don't have a reservation."

"But surely, Miss Bramblett, if I supply you with references and pay for telegrams to check on them, you could make an exception. The men you put aboard the train should have left a vacancy."

Cherry was puzzled by his insistence, and as she studied him she saw a faint touch of red in his gaunt cheeks.

"Miss Bramblett, more than anything in the world I want to meet your grandfather, Judge Gavin Bramblett," Jonathan admitted frankly.

Cherry stiffened slightly and her eyes cooled.

"If you have some sort of legal problem you want to discuss with Gran'sir, Mr. Gayle, he has retired from the practice of law," she told him. "There are a couple of very good lawyers in Mountain City."

Jonathan's grin was thin-lipped and without mirth.

"There are three of them now," he told her. "That is, if I may make so bold as to call myself a very good lawyer. I've put in a number of years trying to be one."

"Then why should you want to meet Gran'sir?" Cherry asked.

"Because I admire him intensely," Jonathan answered earnestly. "I have read a number of his decisions; I've heard a lot about him. I think perhaps his advice might help me to make a very important decision about my own future in law. Besides, I badly need a vacation and I love fishing. So how about it, Miss Bramblett?"

"Well, I don't know." Cherry hesitated, touched in spite of herself by the man's plea. "Gran'sir was badly hurt a few years ago in a hunting accident. He is confined to a wheel chair, and my sister and I try to see to it that he is not disturbed or upset."

"I promise not to do anything that could possibly upset him," Jonathan assured her. "I'll just fish and loaf and pick up any pearl of wisdom he may let fall. And I'm sure there will be plenty of them. He's that kind of man."

Cherry was scowling in bewilderment.

"To hear you talk, one would think Gran'sir was another Clarence Darrow," she protested.

"To my mind, his is one of the most brilliant legal minds in the country, and I am hoping very sincerely that he will write a book for the guidance of young lawyers just getting a tow hold in the profession," Jonathan told her eagerly. "We all go into it with a lot of high ideals that sort of get

5

tarnished as we go along. I know that Judge Bramblett's book would keep the ideals bright and shining."

"Yes," said Cherry. "Drive back with me and stay the night, and then we'll see. You may not want to spend your vacation at Crossways after you've seen the place, though you'll find Gran'sir everything and even more than you expect. He's just about the greatest!"

"Of course," Jonathan seemed to think that was an unnecessary tribute. "And it's very kind of you to allow me to meet him. It's a great privilege."

Cherry studied him for a moment, and then she chuckled disarmingly.

"That should make any further question of references unnecessary as far as you're concerned," she said mockingly as she led the way to the car.

As Jonathan was stowing away his bag and his fishing gear, another car slid to the edge of the parking apron and a tall, sun-tanned, powerful-looking young man leaped out and came

6

hurrying to greet Cherry.

"Hi, there, Cherry! I had a hunch when I woke up this morning that something nice was going to happen to me, and now it has," he told her happily.

"Hello, Job," Cherry smiled at him so warmly that Jonathan looked swiftly from her to the tall young man. "This is Mr. Gayle, who is going up to the Lodge to meet Gran'sir. Mr. Gayle, this is Job Tallent. He's with the forestry service."

The two men shook hands, each taking the other's measure.

"Planning to be here long, Mr. Gayle?" Job asked politely.

Jonathan smiled disarmingly.

"That depends on Miss Bramblett," he answered. "If I can assure her I'm a respectable citizen and not likely to do some foul deed, I hope to spend a vacation at the lodge."

"He's a lawyer and wants to meet Gran'sir," Cherry explained.

"Well, naturally," Job agreed. "Who

7

wouldn't? The Judge is one of the area's most beloved citizens."

"And famous all over the country," Jonathan said quietly.

Cherry and Job stared at him in obvious surprise.

"Oh, come now," Cherry protested. "Flattery's all very well, but how could Gran'sir be so famous and his own family not know about it?"

"If he wasn't, how would I be likely to hear about him in Chicago?" asked Jonathan quietly.

"What's that about a prophet being without honor in his own country? Gran'sir's been holding out on me," she said. "I'll have to have a talk with the man! Shall we get started, Mr. Gayle?"

"By all means," said Jonathan, and once more shook hands with Job and got into the car.

"See you at seven, Cherry?" asked Job. "It's 'romance night' at the movies, remember?"

"Oh, so it is." Cherry grinned

impishly. "Come to the lodge for dinner, Job, and we'll take off from there."

Job returned her grin, and there was a twinkle in his blue eyes.

"It never fails," he told Jonathan in the tone of a conspirator. "I invite her to 'romance night' at the movies and she invites me to dinner at the lodge."

"Sounds like a very good deal," Jonathan agreed.

"Our local movie plays Westerns and 'shoot 'em-ups' five nights a week and then on Monday night they cater to the more romantic-minded," Job confided, and turned his eyes to Cherry with a look that brought color to her lovely face. "See you at six-thirty then, Cherry."

He stepped back and lifted his hands as Cherry started the car and drove out along the town's one main street that led to the mountains.

Jonathan took off his hat and tipped his head back to breathe deeply of the crisp, fresh air. Cherry stole a glance at him, but the road required all of her skill and attention, and she did not look again until they had come out of a dense growth of pines to a sort of shelf above the valley. There she brought the car to a halt. When Jonathan looked at her she grinned and spread her hands, palms upward.

"I always like to watch the tide of spring creep up the mountain. I'm not sure whether it's for the car's sake or mine that I always stop here for a breather. I'm afraid people think I'm completely kooky, since I've lived up here practically all my life, but I never get tired of it. Every few days you can see the tide has crept a little higher. Down in the town it's already spring. But up here you'd think it was still winter, except that every now and then you can see a little more green. And then the dogwood and the wild azaleas begin to show up; and later the rhododendrons are a sight to behold, and everything is green and spring is in full flood."

Jonathan watched her vivid, lovely face and saw the enchantment in her eyes. Suddenly, as though feeling his eyes upon her, she made a little awkward movement and color came into her face as she looked up and met his eyes.

"I suppose *you* think I'm a kook, too," she accused him defiantly.

"I think you are the loveliest, the most charming and delightful girl I've ever had the privilege of meeting," said Jonathan slowly and with such a depth of sincerity that her eyes widened a little as she looked up and met his steady gaze.

Her eyes were more green than gray at that moment, and a brisk breeze ruffled the soft masses of red hair beneath the controlling green ribbon that held the curls in place.

"Well, now, really," she stammered, and was confused and annoyed to hear the faint catch in her breath, "that's

11

rather laying it on with a trowel, Mr. Gayle. Shall we get going?"

Without waiting for his answer, she started the car.

"If I've offended you, Miss Bramblett," Jonathan began, "I didn't mean to be fresh. It's just that I'm a bit groggy from all this fresh air and the beauties of nature, and that 'tides of spring' seemed so apt and delightful."

"I talk too much," Cherry interrupted brusquely, and sent the car ahead as fast as the narrow, steeply winding trail would permit.

"I'm sorry," said Jonathan quietly.

"Sorry?" She was elaborately surprised, airy brows arched.

"Sorry that I destroyed your lovely mood of welcome to the tides of spring," Jonathan said frankly.

"Oh, that!" Cherry shrugged shoulders hugged by her bulky jade-green sweater. "I do a lot of 'nature girl' chattering. Can't help it. Gran'sir brought Loyce, my sister and me up here when we were orphaned. Gran'sir loved this place, but

I suppose he felt that it would be lonely for two small girls, so he tried to teach us to be nature lovers and to find excitement and pleasure all around us. We did, too. Neither of us could ever dream of living anywhere else.

Suddenly the lodge appeared before them. The house was a glorified log cabin. Built of peeling logs that had weathered to a mellow golden color, it stood serenely at the top of the mountain. Fold after fold of blue mountains faded away in the distance behind it and on either side. There was a wide verandah furnished with solid-looking rustic furniture. The windows were wide, and there was a large expanse of sloping, terraced lawn in front. At the left an apple orchard sloped away, the limbs of the trees furred with small pearly-pink buds. On the right there was a garden, neat and trim behind a low stone fence. Beyond the house at the back were the usual outbuildings, and from somewhere there came the sound of chickens and geese, the gobbling of turkeys, and the low mooing of a cow.

Jonathan looked about him and drew a deep breath as Cherry stopped the car and slipped from behind the wheel. A woman clad in blue jeans and a dark sweater, a scarf tied over her head, came up from the direction of the barn, and Cherry called to her.

"Come and meet our new guest, Loyce," she called.

Startled, the woman lifted her head and looked sharply at Jonathan and then at Cherry as she came forward with obvious reluctance.

"You weren't supposed to bring a guest back, Cherry," she protested. "There are no reservations until next weekend."

"Mr. Gayle wanted very much to meet Gran'sir and had traveled all the way from Chicago for just that purpose, and I couldn't refuse to let him ride back with me," Cherry explained. And then to Jonathan, "Mr. Gayle, my sister, Loyce."

"How do you do?" said Loyce frostily.

"I promise I'd go away as soon as I'd met the Judge if you found my presence unwelcome," Jonathan said stiffly, irritated at her manner.

"That will be for Gran'sir to say," Loyce told him coolly, and walked into the house.

Cherry drew a deep breath and turned to Jonathan apologetically.

"I'm sorry Loyce was rude, Mr. Gayle," she apologized. "She's never reconciled herself to the place being turned into a hunting and fishing lodge. After all, it's our home and she thinks we should have privacy. But Gran'sir feels that since the creek has been stocked with rainbow trout and the hunting is so good, we have no right to be selfish with it."

Jonathan nodded. "That sounds like the man I want so much to meet," he said quietly.

Cherry looked up at him and smiled.

"Then come along inside and meet

15

him," she invited, and led the way up the wide, shallow steps, across the verandah that was floored with native stone and into the house.

They entered a huge living room that took up one whole side of the house. There were panels of glass that could be pushed back in warm weather. Today, since there was still a nip in the air, the panels were closed. An enormous double fireplace occupied the center of the room, and there was a vast stone chimney above each fireplace. There was a big fire of logs blazing in one fireplace, and despite its size the room was pleasantly warm.

A man whose thick white hair matched a clipped white moustache sat in a wheelchair beside the fireplace, a book open on a reading stand across his knees, which were covered with a thin plaid blanket.

He looked up as Cherry came in, and his thin, white face was touched with a welcoming smile that faded slightly as he saw Jonathan behind her.

"Oh, there you are, my dear." His voice still held a hint of the depth and richness that had been such a professional asset.

"Gran'sir, this is Mr. Jonathan Gayle, who has come all the way from Chicago for what he calls the 'privilege' of meeting you," Cherry told him severely. "Seems from what he says that you're a very famous guy. How come you never told me?"

The judge chuckled as he held out a thin hand to Jonathan, his blue eyes twinkling.

"How do you do, Gayle? In future, young lady, I trust you will accord me the respect due me."

"Whoosh!" scoffed Cherry inelegantly. "Which would you rather have: my respect, or my undying adoration?"

"I don't suppose it would be possible for me to have both?" asked the judge cautiously.

Cherry thought about that one for a moment while Jonathan looked from one to the other, not quite sure whether they were really as serious as they seemed.

"Um, well, now, I don't know!" Cherry drawled. "Respecting somebody means you're just a teensy-weensy bit afraid of them. Adoring somebody — well, that's different."

"Don't pay any attention to her, Gayle," said the judge cheerfully. "She's a scatterbrain and a disrespectful little minx. But she's a nice child at heart."

"I'm sure she is, sir," Jonathan answered hastily, and flushed as Cherry threw him a mocking glance.

"Well, Gran'sir, do we let him stay or do we toss him out?" she asked her grandfather. "He hasn't a reservation and he hasn't a reference, and we are always most particular about demanding both from our prospective guests."

"I can furnish all the references you could possibly want," Jonathan protested, nettled by the girl's manner.

"I'm sure you can, Gayle," said the

18

judge soothingly. "I told you to pay her no mind. How long are you planning to stay?"

"All summer, sir. That is, if I may?" There was frank anxiety in Jonathan's tone.

The judge's bushy eyebrows went up slightly.

"You're not retiring from the practice of law at your age?" he protested.

Jonathan hesitated. And then he answered quietly, "I'm not sure, sir. I want a few months of quiet and peace in which to make up my mind."

"Disillusioned with the legal profession, son?" asked the judge gently.

Jonathan hesitated and his jaw set hard.

"A little, sir, I'm afraid," he admitted.

"How old are you, son?" asked the judge.

"Twenty-six, sir."

The judge nodded, sighed and glanced at Cherry.

"Run along and get a room ready for

our new guest, chick," he ordered.

As Cherry turned, Jonathan said anxiously, "I hope you don't mind?"

Cherry glanced at him. "Why should I? Gran'sir is the boss. If he says you stay, then you stay."

"I wouldn't want to stay if it would upset you or your sister," Jonathan assured her earnestly.

For a moment Cherry eyed him, and then she smiled; a smile that lit her lovely face and put a sparkle in her eyes.

"It won't," she drawled, and walked away and up the stairs.

"Sit down, son," she heard the judge say, "and tell me about it."

She went down the corridor that bisected the guest wing upstairs, and a pretty, buxom girl in a blue uniform beneath an immaculate white apron called to her through an open door.

"Hey, Cherry, this room all right for the new boarder?"

Cherry paused in the doorway and surveyed the small but cheerfully furnished room — a corner room with windows that looked out over the bold sweep of the mountains and the rushing creek below.

"Well, why wouldn't it be? The best room in the wing," Cherry answered. "After what he's had in Chicago he ought to be tickled simple with this. Here, let me give you a hand."

"Well, now that's neighborly of you," laughed the other girl. "Just check on the clean towels in the bathroom. I've already made the bed fresh and added an extra blanket. Who said it was spring? It gets real nippy up here at night."

"Makes the fish bite better." Cherry laughed. "I hope your mother didn't mind my bringing up a new guest when she had expected to have the next few days free of guests."

"Oh, shucks, you know Muv. The more the merrier. How that woman loves to cook is something I'll never understand. She's going to make things tough for me if I ever find a man of my

21

own and he expects me to be the cook she is!"

"Give yourself time, Elsie m'girl; you'll learn." Cherry grinned.

A tall, rangy man who could have been anywhere from thirty to sixty, judging by his looks, appeared at the end of the corridor, laden with Jonathan's luggage, and grinned bashfully at Cherry as he sidled in to the room and put down the bags and the elaborate fishing gear.

"Figger this fellow's aimin' to catch hisself a real mess o' fish," he drawled as he eyed the gear. "Maybe somebody better tip Job off to see to it fellow don't catch no more'n his legal limit."

"Job met him this morning, and I've got a date with Job tonight, so he'll have a chance to tip Mr. Gayle off to what is the legal limit," Cherry answered.

"You reckon fellow'll be needin' a guide, Miss Cherry?" asked the man hopefully.

"I imagine so. Eben, and I'll tell him

about you," Cherry promised.

"I'd appreciate that, Miss Cherry," Eben answered gratefully as he left the room.

Cherry followed him downstairs.

The judge and Jonathan were deep in earnest conversation, and Cherry paused only long enough to say, "Your room is ready, Mr. Gayle. It's the corner room at the end of the corridor. Go up when you are ready."

She smiled at them and went on out of the house and into the warming sunlight, scarcely pausing for Jonathan's thanks.

2

CHERRY went down the drive around the house and on to the barn. She slid open the big door and saw, at the far end of the building, Loyce bending above a big incubator from which came the cheerful cheeping of newly hatched baby chicks. Loyce was lifting them in gentle hands, transferring them to a big brooder and removing the emptied shells from which they had emerged.

She looked up from a kneeling position as Cherry came toward her, and slid the last handful of newly hatched babies into the brooder before she rose.

"They hatched about ninety per cent," she said happily. "Isn't that wonderful?"

"No more than I would expect from eggs produced by chickens you have raised honey," Cherry told her with a fond smile. "You work yourself half to death looking after them. The least they can do is hatch and grow up and make toothsome yellow-legged fryers for the lodge."

"That man you brought back from town" — Loyce ignored Cherry's words and changed the subject so abruptly that it was like a slap in the face — "I suppose he's staying?"

"I'm afraid so, Loyce," Cherry answered. "He and Gran'sir are hitting it off like two kittens in a basket on a cold night. Gran'sir's calling him 'son' and they're sitting with their heads together and talking up a storm."

Loyce stood for a moment above the feed she was carefully mixing for the afternoon feeding of the poultry. She seemed to have forgotten what she was doing, and for a moment there was a lost look on her thin face.

"Like Weldon and Gran'sir?" she murmured barely above her breath.

Before Cherry could answer, she had

jerked herself back to the present and once more was absorbed in mixing the feed.

"Well, of course if Gran'sir wants him here, there's really nothing you and I can do about it, is there?" she said over her shoulder.

"I'm afraid not," Cherry answered, and added in a little rush, "Loyce, he's really very nice. I think you'd like him if you gave yourself the chance."

Loyce flung her a bitterly derisive glance. "Really?" she drawled. "Run along now. I've got work to do. I'll see your handsome new guest at dinner."

She lifted the huge pan of feed, placed it on a wheelbarrow and trundled it down the length of the barn toward a door that opened out into the chicken yard.

Cherry stood where she was and drew a deep breath. What had happened to Loyce in the fourteen months since her fiancé, Weldon Hammett, had died in a plane which had crashed in a fog on a lonely mountain? All aboard had died in the flaming wreckage.

Weldon had been a minor attaché in the British embassy in Washington and had come to Atlanta to take part in the wedding of a former college friend. After the wedding festivities were over, Weldon and two of the other ushers had come up to Crossways Lodge for a Thanksgiving weekend of hunting before Weldon's return to Washington.

Weldon and Loyce had clicked from their first meeting. Weldon had come back several times for weekends, and then he had asked Loyce to marry him. And Loyce had been transformed from a shy, retiring girl to a radiant, sparkling one.

The two girls had gone to Atlanta to trousseau-shop. The lodge had been in a furor of excited preparations for the wedding. And then the plane bringing Weldon south had crashed and burned just a few days before the date set for the wedding.

Loyce had collapsed from shock and

stunned grief. She had finally rallied, more withdrawn, more aloof, more locked up within herself than ever before.

Cherry heaved a deep sigh and pushed the memories away from her as she turned to go back to the house.

The judge and Jonathan were still deep in conversation, and she did not disturb them. She had work waiting for her in the small library off the main living room, where she settled herself and put the thought of everything else out of her mind.

It was not until lunch time that she returned to the living room. Jonathan sprang to his feet at sight of her, and the judge smiled at her.

"This is quite a lad you've brought me, chick," said the judge. "We've been having quite a chin-wagging session."

"I know, darling." Cherry smiled at him fondly. "Now let's have lunch, and then you must take your nap."

She placed her hands on the back

28

of the judge's chair and wheeled it across and into the dining area of the farther end of the huge living room. The fire on that side of the fireplace had not been lit, but the sun was high now and spilled its warmth through the wide glass panels that framed the magnificent view. A table had been laid for three. As they settled themselves, the judge glanced around the table and at Cherry.

"Loyce isn't joining us for lunch?" he asked wistfully.

"Afraid not, darling," Cherry answered. "She's getting some baby turkeys settled down and planting the south field with Joe and Mart. But she'll be in for dinner."

"My other granddaughter," said the judge to Jonanthan.

"They met when Jonathan first arrived," said Cherry briefly, and looked up as a stout, middle-aged woman in a neat calico dress and a voluminous checked gingham apron shouldered her way through the swinging door from the kitchen. "Muv, this is Mr. Gayle. Jonathan, this is the core and heart of the lodge's domestic arrangements: Mrs. Mitchell."

"Howdy, Mr. Gayle," said Mrs. Mitchell, and began serving the contents of the large, heavily laden tray she was carrying. "I'm right sorry, Cherry, that I have to give you fried chicken, but there wasn't time for anything fancy. I'll give you something special for supper, though."

"Blasphemy!" Cherry protested as she eyed the laden platter of golden-brown, deliciously crisp fried chicken and the platters of vegetables with which it was surrounded. "As if your fried chicked weren't just about the most special thing in the world."

Mrs. Mitchell's broad, ruddy face was touched with a pleased smile.

"I hope you like fried chicken, Mr. Gayle?" she asked anxiously.

"I've never eaten any like this, but I don't see how anybody in his right mind wouldn't be crazy about it,

Mrs. Mitchell," Jonathan assured her earnestly.

"Well, now, that's right kind of you, Mr. Gayle. Soon as you catch a nice mess of rainbow trout, I'll show you what I can do with them," Mrs. Mitchell promised him, and went out of the room, the door swinging smartly behind her.

"Salt of the earth and a treasure beyond compare," Cherry assured Jonathan as she dug into the food before her with the unashamedly hearty appetite of the young. "Muv and her family just about make the lodge possible, don't they, Gran'sir? Her two daughters are the maids; her two nieces come twice a week to do the laundry; her son supervised the dairy and her husband is head guide."

Jonathan said, awed, "Seems you've got the servant problem licked!"

"Servant problem?" Cherry seemed surprised. "Oh, the Mitchell's aren't servants. They're sort of partners in running the lodge. Loyce and I went

31

to school with the two Mitchell girls and the Mitchell son. We could never have started the lodge without them, could we, Gran'sir?"

"Well, I'd hate to have tried," admitted the judge with a twinkle.

"The more I see of the lodge the luckier I feel to be here," said Jonathan.

After lunch, when the judge had been settled for his nap and Jonathan had gone up to his room to unpack and change into something less citified than the garb in which he had traveled, Cherry went back to the small library and the job of settling reservations for the following weekend.

It was not until dinner time that they all met again. Loyce, neat and trim in simple printed silk, her chestnut-brown hair brushed smoothly into a knot at the back of her head and her thin face guiltless of makeup, took her place.

Jonathan tried to be as entertaining as possible, and Loyce was polite if distant in her responses. However, Cherry and the judge were delighted with Jonathan's efforts, and there was a good deal of laughter that seemed merely to brush past Loyce and make no impression at all on her.

Jonathan was recounting an adventure in Washington when the name 'Weldon Hammett' crept into the story. Suddenly Loyce went rigid and stared at him.

"*What did you say?*" she asked huskily, and the tone of her voice was such that Jonathan turned to her, startled.

"Oh, I was probably being a bore," he apologized awkwardly. "I was just telling a story about a cocktail party."

"You said Weldon Hammett." Loyce's husky tone was touched with accusation.

"Yes, a very decent fellow I met at the party, who mentioned the lodge," Jonathan answered.

"You knew Weldon?" Loyce's voice was thick, barely above a whisper.

Jonathan looked swiftly from Cherry to the judge and back to Loyce, scowling in bewilderment.

"Why, yes. I met him a couple of times," he answered.

Abruptly Loyce thrust back her chair and went at a stumbling run out of the room and up the stairs.

Jonathan stared after her and then looked at the others.

"Did I say something wrong?" he asked, bewildered.

"Loyce was engaged to be married to Hammett, and three days before the wedding date the plane that was bringing him south crashed and burned in a fog. There were no survivors," said the judge quietly.

Jonathan was appalled.

"I didn't know," he stammered miserably.

"Well, of course you didn't," Cherry gave him a comforting smile. "How could you, if you only met him a couple of times?"

"I barely knew him, of course," Jonathan mumbled. "He had just come back from attending a wedding in Atlanta and was making quite a story out of his experience here: the rainbow trout that were so hungry in the spring that you had to hide in order to tie your fly; the hunting that was out of this world. Naturally he said nothing about being engaged to a girl here."

"He probably wasn't when you met him, if he'd just come back. He was here for the Thanksgiving weekend to hunt, that was when he and Loyce met. But they didn't get engaged until the following spring," Cherry told him. "You mustn't feel so bad, Jonathan, really. You couldn't possibly have known."

There was the sound of a car in the drive, and she jumped up.

"Oh, that's probably Job," she announced. "I invited him to dinner but I suppose he had to run down a camper's fire somewhere and got delayed. He can have coffee and dessert, anyway."

As she passed Jonathan she patted his shoulder lightly, as if comforting a grieving child, and ran out to the front door.

There was a murmur of voices and then she came back, her hand tucked through the arm of the man Jonathan had met at the station that morning.

"Well, well, Job, nice to see you." The judge shook hands. "I believe Cherry said you and Mr. Gayle met at the station this morning."

The two men exchanged greetings and Cherry said, as she cleared Loyce's place for Job, "You've missed dinner, my friend, but you can have coffee and hot apple pie with 'rat-trap' cheese and make-do with that!"

From the doorway Mrs. Mitchell said firmly, "He can have his dinner. Man works hard like Job Tallent's got to be fed. I'll fix you a plate, Job."

"Muv, I thank you," said Job warmly. "Nice to be appreciated."

Job grinned at Jonathan with a friendly warmth that did not quite mask the faint wariness from his eyes. "Here just for the weekend?"

"Well, no. The judge has said I may stay a month, if I behave myself," Jonathan answered.

"Oh, a vacation, eh? Well, I must say you've chosen a fine place for it, if you really are a dedicated fisherman. There's not much else to entertain a city man, I'm afraid," Job told him.

"Oh, I don't expect to be a bit bored," Jonathan assured him, and for a moment the two men looked at each other and each seemed to take the other's measure.

When Cherry and Job were ready to leave, Cherry said, "Why don't you come with us, Jonathan? It's usually a pretty good movie on 'romance nights'."

Job shot her a resentful glance and Jonathan, perfectly aware of Job's resentment, smothered a grin.

"He probably saw it months ago in Chicago, Cherry," Job spoke up.

"I doubt that," said Jonathan smoothly, and saw the spark that loomed for a moment in Job's eyes.

"I'm not a movie-goer. But thanks for the invitation. Some other time, if I may take a rain check."

"Of course," said Job with false heartiness. "Any time at all. We'll find you a date and make it a foursome. Ready, Cherry?"

"I'll just run up and say good night to Loyce," Cherry suggested.

"Hutch won't be here?" asked Job.

"He's working on that murder case and is pretty well tied up," Cherry said over her shoulder as she went running lightly up the stairs.

The door to Loyce's room stood open, and it was dark save for panels of cool moonlight that spilled through the windows. Cherry switched on the light, saw the room was empty and stood for a moment looking about her. Loyce had gone for a walk in the moonlight. After a moment she put out the lights and went back down to the others.

"See you soon, Gran'sir," she told him as she dropped a light kiss on his cheek, smiled at Jonathan and accepted the coat Job dropped about her shoulders.

The judge watched them as they went out of the house.

"Fine boy, Job," commented the judge. "He and Cherry have known each other since they were children. I liked Weldon Hammett, but I couldn't help wishing he and Loyce had known each other a little longer. Love should have time to mature and ripen, I feel; but that's probably an old-fogey notion that is no longer valid."

"I can't feel that it is, sir," Jonathan told him earnestly. "Most of the divorce cases our firm handles seems to bear out your theory."

The judge studied him for a moment, then sighed and dropped his hands to the chair in which he sat.

"I'm supposed to keep early hours, Jonathan, so I hope you will excuse me if I say good night." He turned the chair with a deft, expert twist and motioned away Jonathan's offer of assistance. "Thanks, no. I can manage.

You'll find books in the library. Make yourself at home with the law books. I've been fifty years assembling them, and it's supposed to be a very adequate collection."

"I'm sure it's far more than that, sir," Jonathan answered as he walked beside the chair to the door beyond the stairs that opened into the judge's own quarters.

As they reached the door it swung open to reveal Eben, tall and lean and whipcord strong, waiting to assist the judge to bed.

"I'll see you in the morning, my boy." The judge wheeled his chair inside the room and the door closed.

3

THE judge and Cherry were already at breakfast when Jonathan came down the stairs, and they greeted him with pleasant cordiality. Eben, gaunt-looking and wearing an immaculate white coat that seemed oddly out of keeping with his rugged appearance, brought Jonathan a glass of frosted apple juice, and Cherry poured his coffee.

"Eggs and toast and ham be all right for you, Mist' Gayle?" asked Eben.

"Sounds perfect, thanks," Jonathan assured him, and Eben nodded and went back to the kitchen.

"Isn't this a perfect day?" Cherry asked gaily, and waved toward the flood of sunlight that was spilling through the windows. "A few days of this and we'll be caught with spring on our hands."

"Do you want a guide, Jonathan?" asked the judge.

"A guide?" Jonathan repeated.

"For your first day of fishing," the judge explained.

"Oh, you don't think I'd better go and get packed?" asked Jonathan.

Cherry and the judge exchanged swift, puzzled glances.

"You've changed your mind about staying?" Cherry asked him.

"I had the feeling that maybe your sister would prefer to have me go," Jonathan admitted frankly.

Cherry's brow cleared and she smiled at him.

"Oh, you mean because you knew Weldon?"

"I didn't really know him. I remember meeting him only once, and I am surprised I even remembered his name," Jonathan answered. "But the mention of his name seemed to upset your sister, and I thought maybe my being here might be unpleasant for her."

Cherry shook her head soberly. "It won't. You'll see very little of her, anyway. She has dinner with the family and the guests. The rest of her meals she has alone."

"She's a very fine girl, Jonathan, and I could wish that she was a bit more outgoing in her attitude toward our guests," said the judge quietly. "She was until Hammett's death. Since then we have made no effort to interfere with the way she wants to live. I can't help feeling that — " He broke off and heaved a deep sigh and smiled faintly. "But after all, I'm an old man and it's been a long, long time since I knew the storm and fury of being madly in love, so I have no right even to think of interfering."

"She would hate our sitting here discussing her like this," said Cherry firmly. "She would consider it an unwarranted invasion of her privacy. So let's talk about something else, shall we? And you are free to stay, Jonathan, until you get bored. Aside from fishing, there isn't really much entertainment up here."

Eben had brought Jonathan's breakfast. Cherry poured him more coffee, and they were pleasantly relaxed and informal. After breakfast Jonathan said, "I'll go for a walk. That's more breakfast than I'm accustomed to, and some exercise is really indicated."

Cherry laughed as she began clearing the table. "Just don't get lost, will you, or fall off a cliff or into a cave. There's a lot of them around, between here and the creek."

"I'll be very careful." Jonathan chuckled. "Least a dumb city man can do is watch his step and not put mountain folks to a lot of trouble getting him out of jams."

"That's a kindly thought." Cherry laughed and started toward the kitchen with a tray laden with breakfast things as Jonathan let himself out of the house.

He went around the lodge and followed a well-worn path toward the outbuildings. The path skirted the outbuildings, and because it wound so steeply down the side of the mountain Jonathan knew that it would lead to the creek, whose brawling sound he could hear as he approached.

He came out on a ledge above the creek and looked down at it. His eyes glistened at the sight. A perfect trout stream.

He was so absorbed in studing the scene before him that he did not hear the breaking twigs that told him someone was climbing the path beyond him.

"Good morning, Mr. Gayle," she said quietly, and Jonathan turned, startled.

"Oh, good morning, Miss Bramblett," he greeted her awkwardly. "I didn't hear you approach."

Loyce nodded, dropped down on a fallen tree trunk and studied him.

"I'm sorry if I was rude last night," she said quietly.

"You were not. I'm sorry that I

45

blurted out a name that upset you."

"Did you know him well?"

"I didn't know him at all. We met once, that's all, at a cocktail party. It was only his mention of the lodge and the judge that stuck in my memory," Jonathan explained quietly.

Loyce sat very still, her hands sunk in her sweater pockets, her eyes on the tips of her scuffed, well-worn boots that were stretched straight out in front of her.

"I suppose there were a lot of beautiful women in lovely clothes at this party?" she asked at last.

Jonathan made a little gesture.

"Oh, you know how cocktail parties are," he answered.

"But I don't," she said quietly. "That's the trouble. I don't know anything at all about what Weldon's life was like. I'm just sure he knew a great many lovely women who were sophisticated and glamorous and all that. That was what worried me."

"It shouldn't have," Jonathan told her gently.

Her smile was so faint that it was little more than a grimace.

"Oh, yes, it should and it did," she insisted. "You see, Weldon was ambitious. He wanted to get ahead as a diplomat. And for a man who wants such a career, a wife is very important — a knowledgeable wife who knows all about important dinner parties and protocol and who sits next to whom at what party, and how to dress and look smart and, most of all, how to talk entertainingly."

"But those are all things you could have learned," Jonathan pointed out.

Loyce nodded, her eyes now on the creek below them.

"Oh, yes, I could have learned. I would have learned all of them, if only I'd been given time." Her voice shook on the last words and she turned her face away. It was convulsed by a threat of tears.

She stood up with swift, fluid grace

and, still without looking at Jonathan, bade him a husky good-bye and went swiftly back up the path toward the house.

Jonathan and the judge had a very interesting afternoon, and at dinner, when Loyce and Cherry appeared at the table, the judge looked so flushed and bright-eyed that Cherry eyed him severely.

"Now see here, Gran'sir, you're not supposed to go getting all excited and wrought up," she reminded him. "It's bad for you, Dr. Williams says."

"Oh, Dr. Williams!" the judge snorted disdainfully. "That old fuddy-duddy! He'd like me just to sit and wither on the vine and blow away. Jonathan and I have had a very stimulating afternoon. Did you know that Jonathan plays a very fine game of chess? He's almost championship caliber."

Jonathan laughed and make a disarming gesture.

"Oh, come now, sir," he protested.

"Did you beat him, Gran'sir?" asked

Cherry with interest.

"Well, yes," the judge said reluctantly.

"And did you deliberately let him?" Cherry demanded of Jonathan.

"Certainly not."

"Then I guess maybe he *is* pretty good at that, Gran'sir," Cherry agreed impishly.

Loyce took no part in the conversation. Yet it was Loyce at whom Jonathan looked most often. However, she seemed entirely unaware of his attention. The moment dinner was over she excused herself and vanished upstairs.

Cherry and Jonathan walked out on the verandah after dinner, and Jonathan told her of his meeting with Loyce that morning.

"I welcomed the chance to tell her how sorry I was that I upset her by mentioning Hammett's name," he said.

Cherry nodded but did not answer.

"She's so lovely that it's a shame she is so unhappy," said Jonathan softly.

Cherry looked up at him in the

moonlight as though startled.

"You really think Loyce is pretty?" she asked eagerly.

Jonathan scowled in puzzlement. "No, not pretty; I think she's lovely. Don't you?"

"Of course I do; I've always thought so. But she doesn't," Cherry answered, and added impulsively. "Will you tell her *you* think so?"

Still more puzzled, Jonathan looked down at her.

"You think she would allow me to?" he asked.

"Oh, yes, of course she would," Cherry said. "I think it would be a wonderful boost for her morale, because she doesn't think she is even good-looking. I think that's the reason she fell so hard for Hammett; he ignored me and made a terrific fuss over her."

She looked up at Jonathan with an expression of guilt that he could sense, though he could not see it in the cool white moonlight.

50

"That slipped out," she confessed humbly. "It's something I've never told anybody. I've felt for a long time that Loyce sort of resents me. Oh, I know that sounds silly, but now that I've started, please let me finish. When we were just babies, people fussed over me and ignored her. I think it was because I was the baby, four years younger than Loyce. I had long red curls; Loyce had chestnut-colored hair that didn't curl. Oh, it sounds so silly! I couldn't believe it until we came here to the lodge. I didn't accept it as the truth after Weldon came. From the very first he made a play for Loyce; and I watched her flower. Now and then she showed signs of being jealous of me; but so far as Weldon was concerned, I didn't even exist. And I rejoiced with all my heart. Everything was wonderful — until three days before the date set for the wedding. And then the world just sort of fell apart for her."

There were tears in her eyes, but she seemed completely unaware of them.

She was looking out over the moon-drenched scene before them and she seemed almost to have forgotten that Jonathan was there.

"Since then there's been nobody but Hutchens Mayfield, who has been in love with her since they were in grade school. So of course a compliment from Hutch wouldn't mean anything to her," Cherry went on after a moment. "But if a good-looking stranger, sophisticated, a big city fellow like you, told her she'd believe it."

Jonathan eyed her curiously. "You'll go to any lengths to get your way, won't you? You'll even spread flattery with a shovel."

Cherry stared at him, affronted.

"Well, of course if you don't want to do it — " she sniffed.

"I'll be glad to, if you think Loyce will let me," Jonathan assured her, "because it's quite true. But you needn't go to such lengths to persuade me."

"Well, of course you'll have to wait

for exactly the right moment," Cherry told him happily.

"I wasn't planning to run upstairs, bang on her door and say, 'Hi, Loyce, you're beautiful,' and then run like the dickens," said Jonathan, somewhat annoyed that she should feel he required so much briefing.

"Oh, you'll find the right moment," said Cherry happily. "And I'm so glad. I've hated to have Loyce feel that she and I could possibly be rivals."

"You're a pretty loyal little somebody, aren't you?" Jonathan's tone was faintly teasing to lift the tension of the moment.

"Where Loyce and Gran'sir are concerned, you bet," Cherry told him firmly.

"Who is this childhood sweetheart of Loyce's? Have I met him?" asked Jonathan after a moment.

Cherry shook her head, the red-gold curls dancing in the moonlight.

"He's county attorney down at the county seat, and there's a murder case about to go to trial that has the whole place in a tizzy. Hutch is working day and night getting things ready. I don't envy him, because the man on trial is a lifelong friend of Hutch's. Yet Hutch has to prove his guilt. It's a terrible responsibility."

"It is indeed," Jonathan agreed. "I suppose the man *is* guilty?"

"Well, the evidence is mostly circumstantial," Cherry answered unhappily, "but it's pretty damaging. The fact that Bob Yorkin is one of the most popular men in the whole county and that the man who was shot was a no-good makes it all the harder for Hutch. Most people in the county think Bob should have a medal for shooting Lafe instead of being tried for murder."

Jonathan shook his head. "If we followed that kind of law we'd have chaos and barbarism back with us," he pointed out.

Cherry nodded soberly. "I know. That's what Gran'sir says. But it's a responsibility I wouldn't want: trying to prove a man guilty or innocent in the face of public opinion."

She looked up at him soberly in the moonlight.

"Was it something like this that disillusioned you about the law?" she asked.

Jonathan's jaw hardened and he looked out over the scene before him, a brilliant mosaic of black shadows and silver moonlight.

"Something like that," he agreed.

4

JONATHAN had slipped into the routine of the lodge until he was accepted like one of the family. He caught glimpses of Cherry during the weekends, very gay and busy and efficient. During the week she relaxed and he had the chance to get better acquainted with her and to come to like her enormously.

Loyce, on the other hand, simply flitted in and out of his sight. She was on hand at dinner, sitting opposite her grandfather, the perfect hostess, polite, gracious but aloof. During the week she was scarcely visible except at dinner, from which she always excused herself as soon as dessert had been served and vanished upstairs to her own room.

There had been no chance for Jonathan to keep his promise to Cherry and to offer Loyce a sincere and honest compliment.

Each day brought the tides of spring closer, and Jonathan spent more and more time just going for long walks, not bothering to fish, simply relaxing, unwinding, not even thinking very seriously about the future.

On a day so perfect that it seemed new-made and fresh, Jonathan walked down through the apple orchard toward the small willow-fringed creek that lay at its foot. Then, so suddenly that he gasped, a terrific clangor broke into the sweet spring beauty of the day.

He had just stepped from beneath a flower-laden apple tree when he saw Loyce beyond him. She was clad in khaki pants and boots, a bonnetlike contrivance over her head and shoulder, her hands covered with stout gloves, and she was beating a steady rhythm with a huge wooden spoon on an old tin pan. And above and through the clangor he heard her raised voice calling to him:

"Stay where you are, Gayle! Still! Don't move!"

Jonathan froze beneath the urgency of her voice and saw that she was standing beside a huge beehive, watching intently as a swarm of bees milled and buzzed about her. She went on making that terrific clamor until finally a small, wedge-shaped mass of bees went into the hive, to be followed a moment later by others, until at least even the stragglers had disappeared inside.

Loyce checked to assure herself that all were inside, then turned and came toward Jonathan, removing the bonnet shaped contrivance that he now saw had a netting web across the face.

"Sorry I had to yell at you, Mr. Gayle," she said coolly. "But I was afraid if you came closer, you might be stung."

Jonathan studied her for a moment as she mopped a perspiring face matter of factly.

"You," he told her quietly, "are a very remarkable woman."

Loyce's brows went up slightly and her smile was faintly touched with mockery.

"Because I can 'hive' a swarm of bees?" she drawled.

"The amazing thing to me," said Jonathan as he walked beside her, "is that a girl so young and pretty as you should be capable of doing so many so-called masculine jobs."

Loyce paused and her brows went up.

"Oh, now, really, Mr. Gayle," her tone was touched with contempt, "that's a very pretty speech but shouldn't you save if for someone more impressionable? Cherry, for instance?"

"It wasn't meant as a pretty speech, Miss Bramblett. It was simply a statement that has been in my mind since the first time we met."

To his amazement, color poured into her face and her eyes went cold.

"I haven't time for this sort of nonsense, Mr. Gayle?" she told him. "And shouldn't you be getting back to the lodge? It's almost lunch time."

"Oh, I'm not expected back for lunch," Jonathan answered, his eyes meeting hers and holding them. "Mrs. Mitchell packed a lunch for me, and I'm planning to find a secluded spot somewhere, eat it and then have a period of meditation. Care to join me?"

"Certainly not," Loyce answered curtly, but he thought he saw a hint of wavering in her eyes that encouraged him.

"I'm sorry," said Jonathan. "I really am. I'd hoped very much that we might have a chance to get better acquainted. You're a very difficult person to get to know, Miss Bramblett."

"Are you sure it would be worth the effort?" asked Loyce.

Jonathan chuckled.

"Now, from anybody but you, I'd say that was a loaded question," he reminded her. "But I'll answer it. Yes, I'm quite sure that getting to know you better would be a tough job but

60

eminently worthwhile. I can't think of anything I'd like better. So why not have lunch with me? I'll share my sandwiches; I'm sure Mrs. Mitchell prepared enough for two."

For a long moment Loyce met his eyes. Her gaze was steady, probing, measuring him; and Jonathan stood quite still and waited. Then suddenly she smiled, and her face was transformed. It became younger, almost impish in its gaiety. She nodded.

"I'm sure Muv prepared enough food for a couple of people, but you must let me provide the drinkables," she told him demurely. "This way, please."

She turned and walked away from him across the orchard away from the lodge. And Jonathan, oddly pleased that he had managed to get even this far past her defenses, followed.

Down a narrow, winding path they came at last to a spot beside a small but very busy waterfall. A huge flat rock offered a resting place, and Loyce walked to the edge of the pool beneath the waterfall, bent and drew up a small rope on the end of which was a quart jar of milk, ice-cold and gleaming frostily. Above the rock there was a hole in the huge tree that leaned above the waterfall, and from the hole she drew out a handful of paper cups.

"I often have lunch here," she explained to Jonathan, amused at his expression. "So one of the men always puts a jar of milk here for me after the morning's milking. Shall we dine?"

Her laughter was soft, faintly touched with uneasiness, as though she had laughed so little that she was out of practice. Jonathan was touched by her gaiety as they seated themselves and she spread the sandwiches on a clean paper napkin on the big rock. And as they ate and chatted he felt that for the first time he was getting to know her a little. She did not talk about herself other than to explain something about the farm operation that provided the lodge with its fresh vegetables, milk, eggs and poultry. She was very casual about it all and seemed to see nothing remarkable in any of her achievements.

"It's not that I do so much of the actual work," she said lightly, "but I have to *know* what should be done so I can tell the men what to do. I get bulletins and leaflets from the Agriculture Department at the State University, and of course the county agent is always glad to answer any questions."

"And what," Jonathan asked quietly, "do you do for amusement?"

She seemed startled by the question.

"Why, there isn't an awful lot of time left over for amusement," she admitted.

"But that's wrong," Jonathan pointed out. "You are a young and beautiful woman."

"Now that's nonsense," she cut in sharply. "I'm neither. Cherry is the beauty in this family."

"Oh, Cherry's pretty and cute and I'm sure she's very popular," Jonathan insisted. "But you are the one who is beautiful."

"You're out of your mind."

She stood up, on the edge of flight, and Jonathan's voice sharpened.

"Sit down. I haven't finished," he snapped.

Too taken by surprise to defy him, she dropped back on the rock, her eyes enormous in her flushed, incredulous face.

"Don't be frightened," Jonathan's tone held more than a hint of mockery. "I'm not going to try to make love to you."

"Well, I should *hope* not."

Jonathan's eyes studied her for a moment, and there was a faint twitch at the corners of his mouth.

"At least not quite yet," he amended, and went on gravely, "Loyce, I'm not being fresh. I do honestly think you are a lovely and very interesting woman and I do want very much to be friends with you. But you wrap yourself in a cloak of invisibility and brush me off every time I try to talk to you. If I'll promise to be very good and not even call you 'darling', will you let me take you somewhere to dinner tonight? There must be somewhere around here that has a bit of atmosphere. Maybe I can borrow Cherry's car."

"We could use mine," Loyce said, and was so obviously startled to hear her own words that Jonathan's pulse jumped slightly. "I mean — that is — well, there *is* a motel ten miles from the county seat that is supposed to have a very good restaurant."

"Then it's a date," he said happily.

"Yes, it's a date," she answered, and put her hand in his as he extended it to help her to her feet.

5

JONATHAN came downstairs a little after six. As he reached the foot of the stairs Cherry came from the den and one glance at her small, woebegone face told him something was wrong.

"Well, come on; tell me," Jonathan urged.

"Loyce sent word a little while ago that she wouldn't be able to get home tonight," Cherry told him. "Queen Lulu is sick."

"Oh, and who is Queen Lulu?" asked Jonathan.

"Our prize cow," Cherry answered indignantly. She added hastily, "Oh, I know Lulu's very valuable and very important. But I don't see why Loyce has to sit up with her. There are the dairy men, and one of them is a graduate veterinarian from the State

66

University. So Loyce doesn't *have* to stay!"

"I guess, then, we have to figure that she thinks sitting up with a sick cow would be more fun than going to dinner with a guy like me," said Jonathan.

"Then she's a fool," Cherry burst out. "Oh, you look just beautiful, Jonny. You don't mind if I call you Jonny, do you?"

Jonathan laughed. "Of course not; it's what all my friends call me."

He was scowling thoughtfully, and Cherry studied him for an intense moment before she offered hesitantly, "I could go with you, Jonny. I'd love to. That is, if you wouldn't mind taking me in Loyce's place."

Jonathan looked down at her flushed, pretty face and smiled warmly.

"Mind? It would be an honor," he assured her handsomely, "if you are sure Job wouldn't object."

Cherry sniffed. "What business is it of his? I'll be right with you, Jonny."

She rushed up the stairs, and he heard the door of her room shut behind her.

He stood for a moment at the foot of the stairs, and then he walked into the big living room where the judge sat reading.

"Come in, my boy, come in," the judge greeted him, and added, "I'm terribly sorry about Loyce breaking her date with you."

"Oh, well, I suppose she thinks the cow is more important, and I'm sure she's quite right," Jonathan smiled. "And Cherry has kindly offered to fill in for her."

"I knew she was going to," the judge confessed. "I'm sorry about Loyce. I admit I had hoped that she might be forgetting her grief about Weldon. She's too fine a girl, too capable, to waste her life grieving.

Jonathan wisely made no attempt to answer. He knew that the judge was merely speaking his troubled thoughts aloud and that no answer was required or expected.

Cherry came down shortly, looking fresh and lovely in a printed cotton dress of jade-green with a beige cashmere sweater swung over her shoulders.

"You look very pretty, doesn't she, judge?" said Jonathan.

"Very pretty indeed," agreed the judge. "Have fun, you two, and don't stay out too late."

"It's a promise, Gran'sir darling," Cherry assured him, and dropped a light kiss on his cheek.

Outside in the cool spring night, she looked up at Jonathan with a touch of anxiety.

"You're sure you don't mind taking me instead of Loyce?" she asked.

Jonathan looked down at her in the moonlight.

"I've known a lot of pretty girls in my time, man and boy," he observed dryly, "but I've never known two with inferiority complexes that could match yours and Loyce's. For Pete's sake, will you please tell me why you should think any man wouldn't be overjoyed to walk into a restaurant wearing you on his arm? Or any other place, for that matter?"

Cherry beamed at him.

"Oh, well, you're a 'big city slicker'," she reminded him gaily. "And I bet you *have* known a lot of pretty girls — all sleek and sophisticated and glamorous. So when you take time out for a backwoods gal like me — "

"In you go before I spank you," Jonathan ordered her. "A backwoods gal my eye!"

Cherry laughed and slid into the car and motioned him behind the wheel.

"You drive," she said gaily. "Anyway, that's why Loyce got cold feet about keeping her date with you tonight. She knew she couldn't compete with your girl friends back home. She and I both know they must be very special."

"Will you accept it as the solemn truth that there isn't one of the girls

I know back home who coould hold a candle to you or to Loyce?"

Cherry considered thoughtfully.

"Well no, I don't believe you, but you're sweet to say it," she assured him.

He eyed her for a moment before he once more gave his attention to the road and Cherry began chattering gaily about people and places and things that made up her interests in the mountains.

The Hilltop Motel was at the junction of the county road with a main north-south highway. It had an oblong of swimming pool in the center, with a cluster of neat-looking white cabins drawn up about it, and the main building a little to one side. Cars were parked in front of all the cabins and the neon 'No Vacancy' sign flashed above the main building that was ablaze with lights. The sound of a jukebox wafted out to Jonathan and Cherry as he parked the car and they crossed the graveled space to the entrance.

The place was well filled. A somewhat harried hostess greeted Cherry by name and welcomed them, even as she cast her eyes about trying to locate an unoccupied table.

From a corner a voice called out, "Hi, Cherry, over here. Couple of extra places, if you don't mind being crowded."

"It's Mabel and Jerry and some of the others," Cherry said happily over her shoulder to Jonathan. The hostess looked relieved as Cherry threaded her way between the tables, crossed the small dance floor and reached the table where a group of six waited.

Jonathan was introduced and made welcome. A waitress produced two more chairs, and everybody moved obligingly to create room enough for two more guests.

"Hi, lookit, Cherry," Jonathan heard the buxom blonde girl murmur to Cherry, "what's with you, palling around with a guest from the lodge? How's Job going to take this?"

Jonathan smothered a grin as Cherry elevated her pretty nose a trifle and answered coolly, "Well, since it's none of his business, why should I give that a thought?"

"Good. Then you won't be upset to learn Job escorted the Widow Marshall to the church box supper Friday night," said the blonde.

Jonathan saw Cherry's eyes flash momentarily, and then she chuckled.

"Well, I always say if you've been to one box supper social you've been to all of them." Cherry answered.

"Is that what you always say?" mocked the blonde. "What I always say: if you've got your claws on a good, steady, dependable boy friend, you are nuts to relax your grip."

"I'm a stranger here," Jonathan murmured in Cherry's ear, "but is it customary to dance while the jukebox blares? If so, would you care to have a whirl?"

"Thanks, I would," Cherry answered, and he thought he detected a note of relief in her voice as she rose and moved with him to the dance floor.

"Who is this Widow Marshall your friend mentioned?" Jonathan asked.

"A very pretty girl who ran away to get married to a man who was killed a few months later in a car crash," Cherry answered. "She came back here to live with her parents. It's absurd to call her the Widow Marshall, for she can't be a day over twenty."

"Any danger that she may undermine you with Job?" asked Jonathan, and added hastily as she flung up her head to stare at him, "Oh, not that it's any of my business, of course. It's just that I didn't want to make any trouble for you by bringing you here."

"I asked you to bring me, remember? And what trouble could it cause? And — oh, hello, Hutch," Cherry broke off as the dance ended and they turned to face a short, stocky young man who showed every evidence of being delighted to see them.

"Hello, Cherry, where's Job?" the man asked, and looked up at Jonathan curiously.

"I wouldn't know about Job," Cherry answered, and her tone said that she was faintly nettled at the mention of his name. "Hutch, this is Mr. Gayle, a guest at the lodge. Jonathan, this is Mr. Mayfield."

The two men shook hands.

"Is Loyce with you?" asked Hutch when the amenities had been disposed of.

"You know better than that, Hutch! When was Loyce ever along on a party?" Cherry said dryly. "She's sitting up with a sick friend."

"Oh? Who's sick? I hadn't heard," Hutch asked with neighborly interest.

"Queen Lulu," answered Cherry.

"Oh," Hutch showed quick concern, "I do hope it's nothing really serious. I know how valuable an animal she is and how attached Loyce is to her."

"I suppose she is," Cherry answered,

and added, "And what are *you* doing out here? I thought you were busily burning the midnight oil, getting ready for the trial of the year."

"I'm seeing someone connected with the case, and yonder he is," Hutch answered briskly. "Glad to have met you, Mr. Gayle. Staying long?"

"A month or so."

"Then I'll probably see you again," Hutch said. And to Cherry, "Tell Loyce hello for me, won't you?"

"Of course," Cherry answered.

"So that's Hutch Mayfield, Loyce's boy friend," Jonathan commented as they made their way back to their table.

"The same," Cherry answered, and added, "Don't underestimate him. Hutch is a nice guy and a brain. He's going places."

"Hooray for him," said Jonathan, and laughed. "Put down that gun, gal. I had no intention of disparaging the guy."

"I'm sorry," Cherry apologized

lightly. "My tongue seems to have been whittled to a sharp edge all of a sudden; I can't think why. Maybe we'd better dance again. That way I can't talk."

6

AFTER lunch one afternoon several days later, Jonathan was going down the path with his fishing gear, intent on an afternoon of loafing and fishing. Loyce was coming hurriedly up the path from the lower field, her head lowered so that she did not see him until she was within a few feet of him. Then she threw up her head and stood rigid, wide-eyed.

Jonathan made no move to allow her to pass. The trail was narrow there and they could not pass unless one stepped aside. And neither did.

Jonathan gave her a slight, mocking bow and said in a tone that was touched with frost. "Ah, the elusive Miss Bramblett, I believe. I do hope Her Majesty is enjoying the best of health."

"Will you please let me pass?"

Loyce's tone was faintly husky.

"In just a moment," Jonathan answered. "First there are a few things I'd like to get off my chest. You haven't given me a chance lately, and I have to take this opportunity to tell you that you are being pretty silly to go to so much trouble to avoid me. It really isn't necessary."

"Don't be silly. I'm not avoiding you. It's just that it's spring and there's an awful lot of work and I've been busy." Loyce hated herself because her voice was not as steady as she wished it to be.

"I'm sure," Jonathan drawled, and added quietly, "What I really wanted to say was that if I grievously offended you by asking you for a date, I'm truly sorry. And if you find my presence here so distasteful, you have only to say so and I'll be off the premises in thirty minutes."

"I wasn't insulted by your asking for a date; that's a silly thing to say. I just couldn't make it, with the Queen ill."

She was stammering. "And as for your presence here being distasteful to me, I only work here, remember? Gran'sir is the boss, and if he likes having you here, then Cherry and I have nothing to say."

"Now that," Jonathan stated flatly, "is a big, fat, colossal lie."

Loyce gasped and her eyes flew wide.

"How dare you call me a liar?" she snapped.

"You know as well as I do that all you have to do is drop a hint to your grandfather that you would like me removed, and it would be done. So make up your mind, my girl. Do I stay? Or do I get a sudden urgent message that necessitates my return to Chicago?"

"You may do as you like," she told him hotly.

"Then I'll stay, for the present," Jonathan told her. "And I'll make you a promise that should ease your mind considerably."

Puzzled, yet curious, she waited uneasily.

"I'll give you my sworn word of honor never to ask you for another date," said Jonathan quietly.

"Well, thanks," she snapped.

"Of course," he went on gently, "should you at any time want to ask *me* for one, I'll take it under consideration."

Loyce caught her breath and sputtered furiously. But Jonathan then merely smiled at her, stepped out of the path, motioned her ahead and went on down to the creek.

Loyce watched him for a moment, and then she turned, her head high, bright color flaming in her cheeks, and went hurrying up the path of the lodge.

Jonathan was infuriatingly matter of fact at dinner, merely rising politely when she excused herself and fled upstairs. Cherry watched him curiously, and soon after the judge and Jonathan had retired to the living room for the chess game that was now a nightly ritual, she went upstairs to Loyce's room.

The door was locked, to her surprise, and she knocked lightly.

Loyce's voice was somewhat muffled as she called out, "Sorry, honey. I think I'm catching a cold. I'm going to bed and try to sleep it off."

"Can I bring you anything?" asked Cherry.

"Thanks, no. I'll be fine. Good night, honey."

Cherry turned away and went back downstairs.

Something had happened between Jonathan and Loyce and it bothered her a bit. She loved her sister and she liked Jonathan, and she didn't see why they couldn't be friends.

She sighed and went on into the library to attend to the day's mail and to bring the books up to date, washing out of her mind anything except the task at hand. When she had finished and came back into the big living room, the judge had gone to bed and Jonathan was alone in front of the fire.

He stood up as she came in and smiled at her, knocking out his pipe.

"Come and relax a bit before you say good night," he suggested, "if you aren't too tired."

Cherry dropped into a deep rustic chair, drew her feet up under her, propped an elbow on the broad arm of the chair, cupped her chin in her palm and eyed Jonathan speculatively.

"I'm just trying to figure out why you and Loyce don't like each other," she said frankly.

Jonathan sobered and answered quietly, "I like Loyce very much. It's pretty plain that she doesn't like me. I'm truly sorry, but I honestly don't know what I can do about it, do you?"

Cherry shook her head, her brows drawn together in an unhappy frown.

"Jonny, I worry about her," she confessed.

Jonathan said quietly, "I know you do, Angel-Face. And it's a shame. But she can't be helped as long as she insists on wallowing in her grief."

Cherry stiffened and her eyes flashed. "I don't like that phrase, Mr. Gayle."

"Don't you?" Jonathan was entirely undisturbed. "Well, what would you call it? A little honest grief for bereavement is understandable. But just to lie down and let it swamp you seems to me a pretty spineless attitude. You mentioned the girl who dated your boy friend Job at the church supper and said she was a young widow. Yet she seems to have made up her mind to go on living, even if her chief reason for wanting to is gone. So why shouldn't Loyce pick herself up, brush herself off, and face up to the fact that life goes on whether we want it to or not?"

Cherry was listening, wide-eyed, unwilling to be convinced, and yet not quite able to resist his logic.

"Believe me, Cherry, I'm not unsympathetic," Jonathan told her gently. "I know she has suffered a great heartache. I'm truly sorry for her. But after all, she is not the only woman who has lost a man she loved. Think of the widows with small children; women whose husbands and sweethearts have died in war, in automobile accidents — Loyce seems to set herself in a niche all by herself and to feel that she alone of all the women in the world has suffered a great loss. And that, my girl, is simply self-pity. And a more loathsome disease I can't think of at the moment."

Cherry was staring at him. After a moment she said uneasily, "But, Jonny, what should she do? She loved him so terribly."

"I'm sure she did, Cherry," said Jonathan quietly. "But what else was mixed up in that love?"

Cherry blinked, puzzled.

"I don't know what you mean," she admitted.

"Simply that this locked-in grief, this withdrawal from the whole human race is very bad for her and, Cherry dear, very dangerous," Jonathan told her.

Startled, Cherry repeated the word, "Dangerous?"

"Mental illness can easily develop, Cherry," he told her with brutal frankness, and saw shock spread over her vivid face.

"Oh, no, Jonny!" she whispered at last.

"Hadn't you and the judge ever thought of that, Cherry?" asked Jonathan. "I would have thought that with all his experience in the legal profession, the many times he must have had to rule on mental illnesses, he would have sensed the danger in Loyce's behavior. But I suppose when it's someone in your own family, you just don't notice — or try not to. There is something there, Cherry, that's intensifying the grief. I think if we could find out what that was and get rid of it, she would get rid of this melancholia that's threatening her."

Cherry was still for a long moment

and then she asked anxiously, "Do you think it's because she works so hard? She does, you know."

"It's not the physical labor that's driving her; it's the darkness inside of her. I thought perhaps if I could get her to go out with me, maybe I could cheer her up; get her mind off her grief. I know that sounds presumptuous as the devil. But honestly, Cherry, it was all I had in mind. I swear it."

Cherry said shakily, "Oh, I know, Jonny. And it was sweet of you. And she was very foolish not to let you. I had fun when you took me out."

Jonathan smiled down at her and suddenly put out his hand and drew her to her feet.

"You're a sweetheart, Cherry," he said, "and I feel like the world's worst heel to have upset you by talking this way about Loyce. But, honey, she needs help and needs it badly."

Cherry was suddenly weeping, and Jonathan's arms drew her comfortingly close as though she had been a grieving child. For a long moment she stood with her face hidden against his shoulder, sobs shaking her body. And then suddenly she felt his arms tighten, his body go rigid.

Startled, she looked up at him and then followed the direction of his eyes to the stairs where Loyce stood, head held high, face white as paper above the shabby dark blue robe that was belted tightly about her slender body. For a moment that seemed to all three of them endless, the tableau held. And then Loyce, still without a word, turned and went back up the stairs, moving on swift slippered feet that made no sound. Not until the sound of her door closing behind her released them from the grip of silence did Cherry speak.

She turned a ravaged, tear-streaked face toward Jonathan and whispered in horror-stricken tones, "Oh, Jonny, how much did she overhear?"

Jonathan was scowling darkly, trying to remember all that had been said and wondering now much of it Loyce had heard.

"I don't know, honey," he said at last, his voice husky. "We were not talking very loudly. But she must have heard more than we wanted her to hear. I know that from the way she was watching us."

"Oh, but that doesn't have to be the reason she was looking so stricken," Cherry stammered, and there was a faint ray of hope in her voice. "It could have been partly because she thought you were making love to me."

A wry grimace touched Jonathan's face.

"Would that thought distress her so much?" he asked.

Cherry flushed beneath the look in his eyes.

"Well, she was afraid I might fall in love with you and that you might not like me that much." Her words stumbled awkwardly.

Jonathan eyed her curiously.

"I hope you convinced her there was

no danger of such a thing happening," he drawled.

"Well, I couldn't," Cherry replied. "I mean I couldn't convince her that I might not fall in love with you. I tried, though — truly I did — because I know how crazy it would be for me to think you could care anything about me."

"You don't say!" Jonathan murmured, diverted from the problem of Loyce by the incredible attitude of the girl before him. "Matter of fact, youngster, it would be the easiest thing in the world to fall in love with you. Only I'm not going to do it."

"Aren't you?" asked Cherry wistfully.

"Of course not, any more than you are going to fall in love with me, you ridiculous child," Jonathan told her. "So that's one problem Loyce doesn't have to worry about, isn't it?"

Subdued, Cherry said huskily, "Well, yes, I suppose it is."

Jonathan looked down at her where she stood, a foot or two away from his arms now, leaning against the tall back of the chair in which she had been sitting. His eyes took her in from the top of her tumbled red-gold curls to the tips of her small feet in scuffed brown shoes. Her sweater and skirt were brown-gold like her hair; a dark green scarf was twisted carelessly about her throat.

"Wouldn't it be ridiculous," he said very softly, "for us to fall in love with each other? You are so much a part of the mountains that you'd die of homesickness away from here; yet all that I have worked for, the whole of my life is in the city. You'd hate it; you couldn't endure it, any more than I could endure a life spent here in the mountains. Don't you see that, honey?"

Cherry set her teeth hard against the impulsive assurance that she could make herself happy anywhere he wanted to live. Instead, when she managed to speak her voice was colorless, without expression, and all she said was, "Yes, of course. Very ridiculous, if you say so."

She turned away then and without another word went quickly up the stairs and away from him. Jonathan stood for a long moment watching the now empty stairs. And then, scowling, he plunged one clenched fist into the palm of the other hand and swore.

7

THE weekend passed without too many complications. On Monday morning, when the last guest had departed, Cherry could relax with the feeling that she had done a good job. It would be five days before there would be another invasion of weekend guests, and she could sit down and worry about her own problems.

Suddenly she turned from the verandah where she had been lingering since the last guest departed and went back into the house. At her desk in the den, she lifted the telephone receiver, called the ranger station and a moment later was talking to Job.

"I've just come up for air after a crowded weekend, pal," Cherry told him with a surface gaiety that was fairly convincing, at least over the telephone, "and I feel a vast need

93

for entertainment. Would you have any ideas in mind?"

"Lots of them," Job told her. "But they're not to be discussed over the telephone, especially with so many eavesdroppers on the line. Hear the clicks?"

"Oh, well, people who have nothing better to do than eavesdrop on my conversations with you are welcome to listen."

"I resent that," said Job huffily. "How about conversations with other guys? Do you mind if they listen in on those?"

"What other guys?" Cherry asked, and felt her spirits rise slightly. "Job, how would you like to take me to the movies tonight?"

"Monday night? Shoot-'em night? I thought you didn't like the 'bang-bangs'."

"I don't, usually. But tonight I think it might be fun to eat popcorn and help the good guys head the bad guys off at the pass," Cherry told him. "Could you get somebody to take over for you tonight? I know it isn't your night off but, Job — please?"

"Honey, when you say it like that, I'd quit the job and kick the boss in the teeth and set a few fires myself," said Job softly. "See you at seven, baby."

"Thanks, Job." Her voice shook slightly.

"Hey," Job's voice was sharp, "are you crying?"

"Good grief, no! What's to cry about?"

"Well, that's better," said Job, and she could hear the relief in his tone. "See you at seven then."

"Make if sixty-thirty and have dinner with us," she invited.

"I thought you'd never ask me." He laughed.

She turned away from the telephone, smiling to herself. Job was a dear. He was mountain folk, as she was. She'd have a good life with Job; they understood each other, and life would be pretty wonderful. And wasn't she the world's prize idiot to go around with her chin dragging on the ground just because a good-looking city slicker had put his arms about her and then told her he had no intention of falling in love with her!

She made herself get up and go briskly about her business.

She and the judge were alone for lunch. When Mrs. Mitchell came in with a big platter of vegetables and a bowl of chicken and dumplings, she announced that Jonathan had asked that a lunch be packed and had said he would not be back until dinner time.

"Chicken and dumplings!" The judge beamed happily. "That looks mighty good after a weekend of trout, doesn't it?"

"I know it's unkind, but let's hope that Jonathan doesn't have too much luck with his fishing. I don't feel I could possibly face another fish dinner tonight."

Cherry said lightly, "Too bad Jonny missed lunch. But then if he wants chicken and dumplings for dinner, Muv will see he gets them."

The judge nodded. "She likes Jonathan," he agreed.

"Do you, Gran'sir?" asked Cherry.

The judge's bushy white brows went up slightly in surprise.

"Of course," he answered as though puzzled she should ask such a question. "Don't you?"

"Oh, yes, I like him," Cherry said hurriedly, and did not quite meet his eyes. "You don't think there is anything shady in his background?"

The judge was studying her with surprised amusement.

"Well, quite possibly there may be," he replied. "I think it's unlikely that any man would reach the age of twenty-five or so without some shadiness in his background. It's in the nature of the male animal to do something along the way that he's ashamed of later on, like maybe getting a speeding ticket or getting into a drunken brawl when he's had four or five over the limit; maybe

97

even pilfering from the petty cash box to put a fiver on the races."

"Oh, I didn't mean anything like that," Cherry protested, flushed and still avoiding his eyes. "Loyce thinks maybe he's married."

Now the judge's eyebrows went even higher.

"Now *does* she?" he wondered aloud. "I can think of only one reason that should be of any interest either to you or to Loyce. And that would be that one of you is about to fall in love with him."

"Oh, Gran'sir, how you *do* talk!" Cherry scoffed.

"I'm quite sure Loyce isn't in any such danger," the judge went on, and now there was no levity whatever in his eyes or in his voice. "I wish to the good Lord that she would fall in love with somebody! Do her a world of good. And as for you — "

"As for me," Cherry cut in swiftly, still not quite meeting his eyes, "there's Job. I have a movie date with him tonight, and I have to do my nails and set my hair and press a dress to wear, so if you'll excuse me, there's work to do and time's a-wastin'."

"All that fussin' just for Job?" the judge asked lightly.

Cherry laughed. "Certainly not. That fussin' is for me. After all, going to the movies is a big event in my life. I want to be properly dressed for it."

He watched her as she went out of the room and up the stairs. Maybe he had been remiss in not questioning Jonathan more thoroughly. Well, he would attend to that tonight after dinner, though he honestly couldn't understand why it should be so important to his two girls whether or not Jonathan was married. They had their two devoted suitors, didn't they? And yet, he admitted ruefully, what did he, an old fussbudget of a grandfather, know about what went on in the hearts of young girls?

Later in the afternoon Cherry went down to the kitchen, the dress she meant to wear that night over her arm. She had pinned her hair up; she wore faded blue jeans and a cotton shirt and her stockingless feet were in battered scuffs. There was nobody in the lodge at that time of day except Muv and Elsie, and informality was the rule.

Elsie was at the kitchen table, elbows propped on it, chin in her hands, her head bent above a somewhat battered movie magazine. Mrs. Mitchell sat in a low rocker beside the open window, beside her a sewing basket out of which she was selecting and sewing quilt pieces.

"Hi, a date?" Elsie asked with interest as Cherry got out the ironing board and plugged in the iron. "With Mr. Gayle?"

"Certainly not," Cherry answered. "With Job. We're going to the movies."

"Oh, no! Not on a Western night!" protested Elsie.

"We're going to help the good guys head off the bad guys at the pass," Cherry answered.

"And for that you're wearing your best dress?" marveled Elsie.

"This old rag?" Cherry sniffed disdainfully as she marveled the yellow-flowered cotton dress over the board.

"That old rag my eye!" Elsie protested. "You know darned well it's nearly brand-new and you haven't worn it half a dozen times."

"Now, Elsie, don't nag Cherry," Muv spoke up. "She wants to wear a good dress on a date, and I admire her for it."

She broke off and leaned closer to the window at the sound of a car in the drive. The next instant a car horn blasted a musical summons.

"Now who in tarnation is that?" she wondered, and glanced at Cherry. "We expectin' a guest?"

"Of course not," Cherry answered.

The horn blasted again; it had a peremptory sound despite its musical tone.

"Well, there's a swell-looking car out there, and a gal drivin' it, and she sure

wants somebody to come a-runnin'."
Muv was at the window now, leaning
close to peer outside. "Must be one
of them tourists from down the valley
that got lost up here. You'd best go
see what she wants, Cherry, before she
ruins our eardrums."

"Scamper, Cherry. I'll finish your
dress," Elsie offered.

Cherry went out the back door and
walked around to the side drive where
the car was waiting: a long, sleek,
impressive-looking white convertible.
The girl who sat at the wheel was
equally long, sleek and impressive-
looking.

She eyed Cherry with a cool,
frosty-blue gaze and demanded, "Is
this Crossways Lodge?"

"Yes, it is."

"Then have somebody get my luggage
out," said the new-comer, and swung
open the door and stepped out on
the drive.

Cherry's eyes widened even as she
took in the slim length of the girl

in snugly fitting cream-colored pants and a matching shirt, a powder-blue sweater almost exactly the color of her eyes swung across her shoulders.

"I'm afraid you've made a mistake," Cherry said when she had mastered her surprise.

"You said this was Crossways Lodge," the girl reminded her curtly. "What an utterly cockeyed name for a hotel!"

"It isn't a hotel; it's a hunting-and-fishing lodge. And the name simply means that it sits crossways on two state lines." Cherry was somewhat nettled at the girl's manner. "And we don't have any facilities for feminine guests."

The girl slid her gloved hands into the hip pockets of her cream-colored pants, cocked her golden head and eyed Cherry with a coolly amused gaze.

"What a racket!" she drawled. "A hide-out for sportsmen but no room for women!"

Cherry's eyes blazed and her cheeks were scarlet beneath the contempt in the woman's voice. But she kept a tight grip on her temper.

"There are facilities for six or at the most eight male guests, and they are middle-aged and dedicated to fishing or hunting or else they wouldn't come to Crossways," Cherry told her. "Now if you will excuse me, there are any number of motels and places where I'm sure you will find comfortable accommodations."

The woman merely eyed her with cool insolence.

"Oh, I'm staying here," she drawled, and turned to lift out a large wardrobe case from the car.

"But I've just finished telling you that you can't." Cherry's grip on her temper slipped slightly.

"And I've just finished telling you that I intend to stay as long as I like," the woman insisted. "That is, if Jonathan Gayle is still here."

Startled, Cherry asked, "Do you know him?"

"Why else would I be here?"

"That is something I wouldn't know," Cherry told her. "But there is no room for you here."

The woman chuckled. "Oh, just put me in the room with Jonny. He won't mind. Or if he does, it won't do him any good. You see, I'm *Mrs.* Jonathan Gayle."

Cherry stared at her as though she could not possibly believe her ears. The woman turned back to the car and lifted out another piece of handsome, expensive luggage, then a weekend case and finally a cosmetic's case. Obviously she was prepared for an extensive stay.

Cherry was still staring at her, wide-eyed, when the woman laughed. And Cherry was suddenly furiously aware of the way she must look in her ancient blue jeans and scuffed sneakers.

"I must say," the woman drawled at last with obvious amusement, "if you are the only competition I have here, I could have stayed safely in Chicago and been quite sure Jonny would come back to me. Now if you'll have someone help me with my luggage and show me to Jonny's room, I'll get cleaned up after a long and tiring drive."

"I'll get one of the guides to look after your luggage, if you'll come this way." Cherry, much deflated, led the way into the lodge, and the woman followed her, bright malice brimming in her blue eyes.

The judge, sitting beside the open window in the living room, looked up as Cherry led the way into the house, followed by the woman who was Mrs. Jonathan Gayle.

"Gran'sir," said Cherry, her voice faintly husky, "this is Jonathan's wife, Mrs. Jonathan Gayle. My grandfather, Judge Bramblett."

She saw the startled look that appeared for a moment in the judge's eyes. But the next moment he was his usual gracious, urbane self as he greeted the woman and made her welcome.

Cherry's eyes widened as she saw the transformation in the woman. Outdoors, alone with Cherry, she

106

had been malicious, contemptuous, generally unpleasant; but here, in front of the judge, she became a different person: sweet and friendly and touchingly respectful.

"I do hope, sir, that you can find a teeny-weeny corner for me, in spite of the fact that this horrid girl says you don't allow women here," she cooed.

"My granddaughter told you the truth, Mrs. Gayle," said the judge, bristling slightly at the phrase applied to Cherry. "Not that we are opposed to women. There are several women employed here at the lodge, including my two granddaughters. But we just do not have the luxuries, the entertainment and the frills that women seem to require."

Mrs. Gayle laughed softly. "The only frill I require, judge, is to be with my husband again," she cooed sweetly, and flashed a glance at Cherry.

"Did Jonathan know you were coming here?" asked the judge. "He hasn't mentioned it, has he, Cherry?"

"Not a word."

"Oh, well," Mrs. Gayle made a little gesture of dismissal "we had a silly little quarrel, and he rushed out of the house in a rage and just sort of vanished. But I love him very much, so of course I took steps to find him. Where is he?"

"Out somewhere fishing," Cherry answered. "He should be back soon."

"Then suppose you have my bags taken up to my room and I'll get freshened up. I can't have him see me all grimy from travel after we've been apart so long, now can I?"

Cherry looked uncertainly at the judge, who nodded. "I'm sure you can find a room for Mrs. Gayle for a few days, honey."

"Of course," said Cherry, and went out.

Behind her as she went up the stairs she heard a burst of soft, silvery laughter from the ravishing golden-haired Mrs. Gayle, and her mouth thinned to a mutinous line.

8

IT was close to dinner time when Cherry came back down the stairs, dressed and ready for her date with Job. There were voices from the living room, and she paused to listen. She heard the judge's amused voice and the light, musical tones of Mrs. Gayle. Leaving by the back door, she headed for the barn.

Loyce would have to be told that Jonathan was not only married but that his wife had arrived!

Just before she reached the barn she saw Jonathan coming toward her in the late afternoon sunset glow. As she saw her he flung up a hand in greeting, and his handsome face, now sun-tanned, broke into a wide smile.

"Congratulate me!" he called. "I didn't catch a single thing, so we don't have to have fish for dinner."

As he came closer he saw her expression and his gaiety vanished.

"Why, what's wrong? Something happened?" he asked in quick concern.

"We have a guest for dinner so maybe you should have caught a trout or two," she said quietly.

"Let him catch his own." Jonathan grinned, but his eyes were still puzzled.

"It's not a 'him'; it's a 'her'. And she loathes fishing," said Cherry mildly. "It's your wife."

Jonathan stared at her, his mouth falling open in complete astonishment.

"My *what*?" he shouted.

"Your wife," Cherry insisted. "Mrs. Jonathan Gayle. She's in the living room with Gran'sir, being very gay and amusing."

"Sandra!" said Jonathan half under his breath. "No one else would have the nerve! Why, that — " His epithet was strangled, but Cherry was sure it was an unprintable word, and in spite of herself her spirits rose a trifle.

"You come with me," he said harshly, and his hand clamped on Cherry's wrist, dragging her with him at a fast clip as he strode up the path toward the house.

Still dragging Cherry with him, Jonathan reached the living room.

Mrs. Gayle, in a stunning formal dress of dark blue chiffon, was enthroned in a big chair opposite the judge, who was watching her with amusement and admiration. She broke off what she was saying as Jonathan and Cherry came into the room.

"Sandra, what the devil are you doing here?" Jonathan's tone was one Cherry had never heard him use before. It had a whiplash sting in it, and she knew that if he ever used it to her she'd simply curl up and die.

"Jonny, darling!" the woman fluted joyously, and ran to him, obviously about to fling herself into his arms. But Jonathan evaded her, holding her off with hands that were anything but gentle. His eyes blazed and his jaw was

111

set so hard that small muscle leaped along it.

"Jonny, dearest, you're hurting me," she whimpered, twisting, trying to free herself from the grip he had clamped on her shoulders to thrust her away from him.

"I ought to break your neck!" said Jonathan in that whiplash voice that made him suddenly seem like a frightening stranger.

"Now, Gayle, there's really no call to use such a tone to your wife," the judge said brusquely.

"My wife?" Jonathan's tone made the two words an epithet. "Sir, she's not my wife, and she's never going to be. I haven't got a wife; and if I did, it wouldn't be Sandra Elliott."

His hands still held the woman, and now he shook her.

"Tell them the truth, Sandra, or so help me, you'll wish you had," he grated, and flung her toward the chair where she had been sitting.

Sandra sprawled for a moment before

she managed to recover herself and once more assume a graceful pose.

"Oh, well, you can't rule a gal off the course for trying," she sneered.

"How did you find me?"

Sandra laughed softly. "Oh, it wasn't easy, darling," she mocked him lightly. "But when a girl is as much in love as I am, she finds ways. Private investigators are expensive, but they are also effective."

"Well, you're leaving here and now. Come on!" ordered Jonathan.

"Oh, the judge has said I can stay for a day or two until I rest up from my long trip," she cooed sweetly. "It was a very hard trip, Jonny darling, and I'm simply exhausted. And I do hope dinner will be ready soon. I'm starved."

She turned her limpid gaze on the judge, and somehow, Cherry could not quite see how, she managed to look young and defenseless and pathetic.

The judge met her eyes for a moment, and then he glanced at

Jonathan and said, "We can't turn her out at this hour of the night, Jonny, without her dinner. I'm sure she'll be quite willing to leave tomorrow. You go wash up for dinner. It'll be ready in a few minutes."

Jonathan glared at Sandra, who looked back at him with a faint smile. And then he turned and stalked up the stairs, passing Loyce.

Jonathan paused for a moment beside her and said huskily, "I wouldn't have had this happen for the world, Loyce. Please believe me."

Loyce merely drew back to allow him to pass and averted her head. For just a moment Jonathan looked at her, and then he went on up the stairs.

The big front door swung open to admit Job, who came like a breath of fresh air into the supercharged atmosphere. Instantly he sensed the tension and stood uncertainly until Cherry came to greet him.

"Come in, Job, and meet our new guest," said Cherry. She tucked her

114

hand through his arm and drew him forward. "Miss Elliott — isn't that what Jonny called you?"

Sandra lifted blue eyes that were smoky with suppressed anger but that lightened somewhat as she saw the lean sun-tanned young man who stood beside Cherry.

"I'm Sandra Elliott," Sandra answered, and gave Job a dazzling smile. "And who are you?"

Cherry said quietly, "Job, this is Sandra Elliott, Sandra, Job Tallent, my fiancé."

Job and the judge both looked startled. Job looked down at Cherry, and his arm, through which her hand was tucked, tightened and drew her closer to him.

Sandra raised her eyebrows slightly, and her laugh was little more than a soft chuckle.

"Serving notice on me, are you?" she mocked. "Putting up a sign, 'This man is mine, so hands off'?"

Job, somewhat dazzled by her charms,

laughed. "I'm delighted to meet you, Miss Elliott."

"Oh, do call me Sandra," she purred, and Cherry ached to slap her as she gave Job the full benefit of her lovely smile. "When people call me 'Miss Elliott', I'm afraid they are bill collectors and I've overlooked paying them."

The judge cleared his throat and held out his hand to Loyce as she came into the room.

"And this, Sandra, is my other granddaughter, Loyce," he said. "Sandra is staying overnight with us, honey."

Cherry saw Sandra's eyes flash at the 'overnight', but she smiled casually at Loyce and said with surface pleasantness, "Hello."

"How do you do," said Loyce with quiet formality, and excused herself to check on dinner.

Jonathan came down, his face a dark thundercloud of helpless anger, and dinner was announced. As they moved toward the dining area, Sandra

116

managed to slide her hand through Job's arm and to walk beside him, looking up at him, twinkling her charming smile.

Jonathan stood grimly watching her, his jaw set and hard.

After dinner, when Job and Cherry were ready to leave for their date, Sandra asked wistfully, "Are you going somewhere that's very gay and exciting and a lot of fun?"

Job said instantly, "Only to town to the movies. Why don't you and Jonathan come with us?"

Cherry caught her breath on a small, soundless gasp as Sandra stood up, bright-eyed and eager.

"Oh, that sounds like fun. Shall we, Jonny, darling?" she asked.

"Certainly not," Jonathan told her savagely. "You aren't going anywhere until you and I have a talk."

Deliberately ignoring his tone, she gave him a melting glance.

"Oh, darling, that sounds like lots more fun than the movies," she responded sweetly.

Jonathan merely glared at her and seemed to fight for a grip of his temper. Cherry said under her breath to Job, "Let's get out of here."

She dropped a light kiss on the judge's cheek, nodded to Sandra and Jonathan, and led the way out. Job paused to say good night to Sandra before he followed her.

Outside in his sturdy station wagon, Job said eagerly, "What a beautiful girl! Who is she? Jonathan's fiancée?"

"He says not," Cherry answered. "She arrived, announcing she was his wife, but he had a fit and denied it."

Job whistled as the car rolled down the steep, winding drive toward the highway. "Well, you'd think any man in his right mind would jump at the chance to marry a beautiful gal like that."

"She's an utterly shameless creature who hired private detectives to trace Jonathan for her and then descended on him like a hen on a June bug!"

Cherry exploded. "Job, do you really like her?"

Job told her. "I've been in love with you since we were kids. When you introduced me as your fiancé, I felt about nine feet tall, because I was hoping you meant it. *Did* you, honey?"

Cherry hesitated for a moment, and then she turned in the seat to face him.

"Job darling, you are my very dearest friend," she told him with deep earnestness. "But I don't know if that's being in love. I'd rather be with you than with anybody else in the whole world. But I don't know if I'm ready to marry you or anybody else yet. Couldn't we just go on being very dearest friends for a little while longer? I'll make up my mind, Job darling, one of these days. Honestly I will!"

Job's face was taut now, his hands clenched on the wheel of the car, his eyes straight ahead.

"I suppose that's as much as I can

hope for, isn't it?" he said at last. "But it's not an awful lot, honey, for a man who loves you as much as I do. Will you tell me one thing, Cherry?"

"If I can," she answered warily.

"Is there anybody else?"

Cherry caught her breath, and her eyes widened. In the faint light from the instrument panel, she felt her cheeks grow warm with color and was glad that he could not see the blush.

"Is there, Cherry?" he insisted when she was slow to answer.

"Why, Job, how could there be?" she asked. "I don't know anybody else."

"There's Jonathan," he said grimly.

"Jonny? Oh, but, Job — why, my goodness! Gracious, Job, you surely don't think I'd fall in love with him!" she stammered wildly.

"Why not?" demanded Job. "He's a darned good-looking guy; and he has the added novelty of being somebody new; somebody you haven't known since you were a kid. It would be easy for a young, impressionable girl to fall for a fellow like that."

"Well, for goodness sake, I haven't," cried Cherry, and wondered if her voice sounded overly emphatic.

9

SANDRA rose gracefully from her deep chair and smiled enchantingly at the judge, ignoring Jonathan, who was watching her with a dark, angry scowl.

"I'm going to run along to bed," she announced sweetly. "It's been a very tiring trip, and there were weeks of suspense and anxiety after Jonny left before my detectives could find out where he had gone. So I'll say good night."

Jonathan said savagely, "Oh, no you won't. We're going to talk."

"Oh, not tonight, Jonny darling, please," she whimpered like a weary child. "I'm so terribly tired, and I have one of my dreadful headaches. You know how they torture me. We'll talk tomorrow after I've had a good rest."

She smiled sweetly, came close and

brushed his cheek with her lips before he could guess her intention and evade her. She chuckled wickedly as she saw his instinctive recoil, twinkled demurely at the judge and went up the stairs.

The two men were quite silent until they heard the sound of her closing door, and then Jonathan said awkwardly, "I can't tell you how sorry I am about this mess, sir."

"What does she want?" asked the judge quietly.

Jonathan hesitated, and the judge added, "Aside from her expressed determination to marry you, I mean."

"Oh, there was never any question of marriage between us, Judge," Jonathan protested with an almost desperate earnestness. "I hope you will believe that, sir. I never asked her to marry me. I never did anything that would lead her to believe that I had any such intention. I dated her now and then. I don't believe she really wants to get married. She has a very good career as a fashion model, and

I'm sure she wouldn't want to give it up."

The judge had listened quietly, and when Jonathan finished, he asked, "So what *does* she want?"

And Jonathan said starkly, "Money."

The judge's eyebrows drew together in a scowl.

"Blackmail?" he asked, puzzled.

"It's a form of that, sir, I suppose," Jonathan answered bitterly. "She seems to feel that if she can worry and harass me enough, I'll decide it's worth a sizable check to make sure she stops being a nuisance. Does that sound logical to you, sir?"

"Painfully so." The judge nodded. "If you are convinced she isn't in love with you, I can't see what else it could be."

"Well, she's not in love with me, believe me, sir, any more than I am with her," Jonathan answered.

The judge was silent for a moment, and then he shook his head.

"An astounding woman!" He sighed.

"Judge, should I try to buy her off?" asked Jonathan.

The judge stared at him as though shocked.

"Pay her off? My dear boy, haven't you been in the legal profession long enough to realize that paying off blackmail is an endless business, especially the kind this woman wants? No, Jonathan, I doubt if you could buy her off and make it stick."

Jonathan nodded grimly.

"That's about the way I had it figured out," he admitted. "I *did* think this time I'd managed to cover my tracks sufficiently to get away from her. Judge, how can any woman be so lacking in pride and self-respect as to hound a man she knows doesn't even *like* her?"

"She would have to want money, a great deal of it, so badly that nothing else would be important," the judge answered heavily.

The two men were silent for a long time, and then the judge asked curiously, "Was this the real reason you gave up your work in Chicago and came down here — just to get away from her?"

Jonathan colored. "Sounds pretty cowardly, doesn't it?" he asked. "Yes, it was partly to get away from her. I was pretty disillusioned with some of the aspects of my profession as it was being practiced in the firm of which I was a junior partner. But I may as well admit that I'd also grown pretty fed up with having her turn up everywhere I happened to be, with her eternal 'Jonny, darling!' and her air of owning me body and soul."

The judge's eyes twinkled. "I can imagine that could get pretty tiresome, even though she *is* a beautiful woman."

Jonathan eyed him sharply. "You think she's beautiful, Judge? I think she's completely hideous," he burst out.

"Under similar circumstances I'd probably think the same," the judge agreed. "Well, Jonny, we may as well get a good night's sleep on it; tomorrow maybe we can view the problem more objectively. At least she will be leaving tomorrow."

"Oh, no, she won't, Judge!" Jonathan burst out. "She's here to stay until I either leave or pay her off. So I'd better go up and start packing."

"Let's wait and see what sort of wisdom the morning brings, Jonny," the judge told him gently. "Good night, my boy."

Jonathan walked with the judge to the door of his own room, where Eben was waiting. And then he walked out of the lodge and to the wide front verandah.

He filled his pipe, lit it and stood for a long moment, scowling as he looked out over the rolling sweep of mountains. The late-rising moon was not yet visible, but the sky was so clear that the millions of stars looked like blazing diamonds caught in a dark web.

He was so lost in his unhappy

thoughts that he was not aware of Loyce until she spoke, from the shadows at the corner of the verandah where she sat curled up in the big old swing.

Jonathan turned, startled.

"Did she really hire private detectives to find you, Jonathan?"

Jonathan walked toward the end of the verandah where she sat. He could not see her in the shadows. She was just a dim blur, her face a pallid oval in the dusk.

"I suppose she did," he responded. "I can't think how else."

"She must love you very much," said Loyce quietly.

"That's nonsense. She doesn't love me at all."

"Then why would she pursue you so shamelessly?"

"If she were really in love with me, *would* she pursue me?"

She sat very still for a moment as though his words had surprised her.

"Why, no," she said softly at last on a note of wonder. "No, of course

128

she wouldn't. She would have waited and hoped and maybe prayed that you loved her enough to come back or to send for her."

"Of course," said Jonathan grimly.

"Then why did she hire private detectives to find you if she was not in love with you? She must know she can't force you to marry her if you don't want to."

"She wants," stated Jonathan wearily, "to make so much of a nuisance of herself by following me, forcing herself on me, that I'll be willing to pay her a handsome sum to be rid of her."

He heard the swift, startled movement with which Loyce sat erect.

"Oh, no, Jonathan, no woman could be that shameless," she protested.

"I'm afraid you don't know women like Sandra," Jonathan told her. "I don't really think there are a great many of them. I surely hope not."

There was silence while Loyce digested that thought, and then she burst out. "But I don't understand. She's so beautiful I'd think any man she wanted would want to marry her."

Jonathan's mouth was a thin taut line.

"You might think so, at that," he agreed without expression.

"Jonathan," asked Loyce at last, and her voice was touched with embarrassment, "could I ask you a favor?"

"Well, of course, Loyce. You know you don't even have to ask," Jonathan answered swiftly. "What is it?"

She hesitated for a long moment, and then she asked, "Will you help me find a private detective who will do a *very* confidential job for me?"

"You want the services of a private detective, Loyce?"

"There's something I *have* to know, Jonathan. And I don't know any other way to learn than to hire a private detective to find out for me," she told him. "I don't suppose there'd be one down at the county seat. And anyway, I'd need one from Atlanta or maybe

130

even Washington."

Jonathan was very still for a moment, and then he asked quietly, "Do you want to tell me about it, Loyce?"

"I think perhaps I would. I have to talk to somebody about it, and I can't talk to Gran'sir or Cherry. They'd think I was out of my mind."

Jonathan waited, and after a moment she said shakily, "I want to know if Weldon really *was* on that plane that crashed."

Jonathan sat erect.

"But, Loyce, if he hadn't been — " he began, and broke off for an instant before he went on more vigorously, "Loyce, it's been over a year since the crash. If Weldon had missed the plane, if he were still alive, he'd have come back. You'd have heard from him."

"Would I?" It was a thin thread of sound that came faintly to him from the swing.

"Loyce, I don't understand," Jonathan admitted his confusion. "You were within a few days of marrying the man; you were deeply in love with each other. Are you trying to say you think he was not killed in the crash and that he has deliberately failed to let you know? You don't have much faith in the man, do you?"

"You see, Jonathan, Weldon had been accustomed to beautiful women like Sandra — women who were knowledgeable about diplomatic affairs, parties, and dinners, and protocol and — oh, a million things I had never even heard of. So when the plane crashed, if he *wasn't* on it, mightn't he have seen that as a way of escape?"

"A way of escape?" Jonathan repeated.

"A way of escape from an unsuitable marriage," said Loyce. "Weldon was very ambitious. He wanted a real career in the diplomatic corps, and he had a wonderful opportunity. His family was rich and socially prominent in England. He had connections; knew the right people."

"Loyce, you are building the most absurd fantasy," Jonathan told her.

"After all, what right have you to dishonor his memory this way? Did he seem, before he left the last time, to be getting tired of the thought of your marriage?"

"Oh, no," she whispered, and for a moment there was a silvery radiance in her voice that wiped out the tears. "He was as dear as ever. He was telling me about the apartment he had found for us. It was in a place called Georgetown, and he said he felt we would be very happy there."

"Then where did you get this crazy idea that maybe he wasn't on the plane?"

She drew a deep, hard breath, and he could see her face lift.

"I just have to know, Jonathan. I've got to be certain beyond any faint possibility of doubt that he didn't just walk out on me," she told him.

Jonathan said sharply, "You've been torturing yourself with this crazy idea ever since the plane crash, haven't you?"

"How could I help it?" she whispered.

"Loyce, don't you know that you can't really love anybody unless you have faith in him? How could you doubt Weldon if you really loved him?" Jonathan demanded sharply.

"I knew how unworthy I was," she whispered faintly.

"So when the plane crashed and there were no survivors, you began to wonder if maybe he hadn't been on the plane and had used the crash as a means of ending things between you," said Jonathan, and had difficulty keeping the scorn out of his voice. "I must say you didn't give him much faith or much benefit of the doubt. I can't understand how you could think such a thing."

"I did and I still do," she told him stubbornly. "That's why I have to know. There are ways to find out if he was on the plane, aren't there?"

"Well, I suppose so. His name was undoubtedly on the flight list."

"And if he wasn't and has been

transferred to another post, the embassy in Washington would know, wouldn't they? He'd have to use his own name."

"This whole thing is so crazy that I find it hard to believe you really mean it," Jonathan told her.

"But I do mean it, Jonathan. I never meant anything more," she insisted stubbornly. "Now do you see why I have to have a private detective, one who can get me proof so that I'll *know*?"

"For your own peace of mind, I can see that," Jonathan agreed.

"And you'll help me, Jonathan?" she pleaded.

"Of course," he assured her, and added curiously, "this is the reason you have crawled off into a hole and tried to resign from the human race, isn't it? I've wondered why you found it so hard to make the adjustment."

"I suppose I've been a fool, Jonathan," she said with a humility he found very touching. "I think I was a little afraid when Weldon asked me to marry him. Oh, I adored him and I was sure he loved me. But when I thought of all the problems we'd face, of myself as the wife of a rising young diplomat — oh, Jonathan, I was scared! I tried to tell him, and he only laughed at me. He didn't seem to mind that I was ignorant of all the things a diplomat's wife would be expected to know. He just said, 'Oh, you're smart, darling. You can learn.' And I would have, too."

"Of course you would, Loyce," Jonathan comforted her. "And I think you should give up this idea that Weldon escaped the crash and ran out on you. I don't believe he'd be capable of a thing like that."

"I don't want to believe it, Jonathan," she confessed. "But, Jonathan, I have to *know*! Else I'll go out of my mind."

Jonathan tensed at the words and instantly realized that they were meaningless, a cliché she had spoken without thought.

"Jonathan, will you help me?" she asked.

"Of course, Loyce," he told her quickly, his voice warm and touched with tenderness. "I'll telephone a friend in Washington tomorrow and have him make inquiries. I'd better go to town and call from the telephone exchange to be sure the call will be private. A party line like this one up here is no good for confidential messages."

"No, of course not." She stood up and swayed for a moment before she could steady herself. Jonathan's hands shot out to steady her, and for a long moment she leaned against him as though completely exhausted. Then she straightened and lifted her head, and he could see, now that she was within reach of the yellow lamplight from inside the lodge, that she had managed a faint, shy smile.

"I'm so very grateful, Jonathan," she told him, her voice shaking. "I don't know how to thank you. I couldn't think of anybody else I could ask; and

I didn't know how to start to do it for myself."

"It will be a privilege, Loyce, to convince you once and for all that any man who had the faintest chance of marrying you would never run out on that chance."

There was more emotion in his voice than he had wanted there. But apparently she was too overwrought to realize it. She only smiled and walked to the door beside him, seeming scarcely conscious that his arm was about her, steadying her.

"You'll go down and telephone tomorrow, Jonathan?" she asked at the foot of the stairs.

"The first thing in the morning," he promised her gently.

"I seem to be rushing you, don't I?" she apologized humbly. "I'm sorry. It's just that it's been so long, and I've been so bewildered and miserable."

"I'll telephone my friend in the morning," Jonathan promised. "But it may take a few days or even longer to find out what you want to know, so you mustn't be impatient."

"I've waited so long, Jonathan," she told him, and there was a touch of radiance in her voice. "I can wait a while longer without getting impatient. Just knowing that something is being done will make the waiting easy."

She stood on the bottom step of the stairs, smiling at him. Then suddenly, impulsively, she leaned forward, brushed her lips against his cheek and, scarlet with confusion, turned and hurried up the stairs.

10

IT was close to ten o'clock the following morning when Sandra trailed downstairs. Every hair was in place; false eyelashes on; her tight pants a blazing orange, her shirt a pink that screamed at the pants. It was a combination of colors that caused Cherry's eyes to widen and that made Elsie, bringing Sandra's breakfast tray into the dining room, choke on a smothered laugh.

"Hi," said Sandra, and eyed the breakfast tray hungrily. "I really shouldn't, but I'm starved. Where's Jonny?"

"He's gone into town," Cherry answered.

"Town?" Sandra's brow wrinkled with disgust. "You mean that horrible little crossroads halfway down the mountain? What could he possibly want down there?"

"I didn't ask him and he didn't tell me," Cherry answered briefly.

For an instant there was a look of alarm in Sandra's eyes.

"He'll be coming back, won't he?" she demanded.

Cherry's brows went up slightly.

"I imagine so. He didn't take any of his luggage, and he's using Loyce's car," she replied.

Sandra relaxed slightly and dug an appreciative fork into the golden mound of scrambled eggs on her plate.

"I'm hoping to get my business with him attended to so I can get away from here in a hurry," she said cheerfully.

"I don't want to be nosy," said Cherry, "but aside from your expressed intention of marrying him, and his insistence that you're going to do nothing of the kind, I can't help wondering just what your business with him is. If I'm not speaking out of turn, of course?"

Sandra laughed, bright-eyed. "Oh, I

don't mind telling you, I'm here to collect some money Jonny owes me; rather a lot of money."

Cherry stared at her.

"You mean you worked for him and he didn't pay you?" she wondered aloud.

Sandra shrugged a shoulder.

"You might put it that way," she said mockingly. "He took up practically all of my free time for more than six months. I lost several good modeling jobs because of dates with him. So I feel he owes me for those missed jobs, don't you?"

Cherry was silent for a long moment, and then she said with an air of relief, "You're joking! You've *got* to be joking!"

"Why?" demanded Sandra, who quite obviously was doing nothing of the kind. "If Jonny likes to be seen in public wearing on his arm a beautiful gal, all done up in the very latest fashion, then he should be willing to pay for the privilege, especially as he is so stinkin' rich he can easily afford twice what I feel he owes me."

Cherry asked, "Jonny is rich?"

Sandra elevated her eyebrows in amused disdain.

"Oh, come now you must have known that all along. Jonny doesn't even count his money any more; he just weighs it. Some aged relative is always shuffling off and leaving Jonny more money. Don't tell me you didn't know that?" she sneered.

Cherry stared at the incredible creature across the table from her. "You want Jonny to give you money just because you missed a few modeling dates to go out with him?" she marveled.

"Oh, of course not." Sandra shrugged. "I expect him to give me fifty thousand dollars so I'll go away and not bother him any more."

She looked across the table at Cherry's shocked face and chuckled as she poured herself another cup of coffee. "I rate it as my nuisance value to him," she drawled. "He knows if he doesn't pay me, I'll turn up wherever he goes and make things embarrassing for him. So-o-o, he gives me a check and I go away. It's as simple as that."

"Simple!" Cherry exploded furiously. "It's the most disgusting, the most completely shameless thing I ever heard of in all my life."

"Really?" Sandra's eyes brimmed with derision. "Oh, well, that's because you've been buried down here in this awful wilderness all your life and don't know anything about what goes on in the outside world."

"Well, if you're an example of what goes on in the outside world, I'll spend the rest of my life at Crossways Lodge and be very glad to do it," Cherry told her hotly.

Sandra studied her deliberately through the thin blue smoke of the cigarette she had lighted to go with her final cup of coffee.

"Of course I'll marry Jonny like a shot if he prefers that to giving me fifty grand," she drawled. "But I have a hunch he'd rather buy me off. And as soon as I get my paws on him, I'll see that he writes me a check and I'll be a long time gone."

She stood up, grinning wickedly at the dazed look on Cherry's face.

"Get smart, chérie," she drawled, "or you *will* spend your life in this gosh-awful place with that primitive male! You're not a bad-looking chick if you'd just make the most of yourself. But of course, as long as you are satisfied with the Job guy and he's satisfied with you, what difference does it make? I'll see you around."

She strolled out of the room, past the huge fireplace that on this warm morning did not hold a fire. The judge was on the side terrace in the sun, and for a moment Sandra hesitated at the big glass doors as though tempted to join him. Then she shrugged and went back upstairs.

The moment she was gone the swinging door into the kitchen burst open and Elsie stood there, wide-eyed and incredulous.

"Cherry, she wasn't joking!" she burst out. "That gal meant every word she said."

"She did indeed," Cherry agreed, and the two girls looked at each other with wide, shocked eyes.

"Cherry, do you suppose Mr. Gayle will pay her off?" asked Elsie after a moment.

"I imagine he'll be glad to," Cherry answered grimly. "Only will she really let him alone if he does?"

"You think if he gives her a check she'll come back later on for more?" Elsie was appalled at the thought.

"Well, what would there be to stop her?" asked Cherry, and make a little impatient gesture of dismissal. "Oh, for Pete's sake, Elsie, we're a couple of dopes even to give it a thought. Jonny knows his way around; he'll be able to handle her."

"Gee, I sure hope so," said Elsie. "He's a right nice man, and I'd sure

146

hate to see him all tied up with that witch! You know something, Cherry? If she's typical of women in the outside world, as she calls it, I guess I'll just settle down here in the mountains and be satisfied."

"That makes two of us," Cherry answered firmly, and helped Elsie clear the table.

Jonathan had not returned by lunch time. Cherry was startled when Loyce came down to the table to join the family.

The judge and Cherry hid their surprise and delight at her appearance, and she plunged immediately into a discussion with the judge about some plans she had for the home fields.

Sandra watched her with a curious intentness, and Cherry all but held her breath, so fearful was she that Sandra would say something that would upset Loyce.

They were halfway through lunch before there was the sound of a car in the drive and Cherry saw Loyce sit up alertly, breaking off in the middle of a sentence as she listened to the sound of footsteps crossing the graveled drive and climbing the steps and then coming on across the verandah.

When Jonathan came into the dining area, Loyce's eyes lit up and a soft surge of color touched her face. Cherry was watching Sandra and saw Sandra watching Loyce; there was an ugly glint in Sandra's eyes. Cherry held her breath, prepared for an explosion as Loyce's eyes asked a question of Jonathan, who smiled and shook his head slightly.

The whole brief scene had lasted no more than moments, and yet Jonathan had brought into the room with him a supercharged atmosphere that tensed Cherry's nerves.

"You're just in time for lunch, my boy," said the judge, and Jonathan smiled his thanks and took the place beside Loyce, which brought him directly across the table from Sandra, who was eyeing him grimly.

"You still here?" Jonathan asked curtly.

Sandra rested her elbows on the table on either side of her plate and put her chin in her palms, eyeing him with a look that held hatred and viciousness.

"Oh, I'll be here for a quite a while," she drawled. "That is, of course, unless you want to send me packing. And you know the only way you can do that, don't you?"

Jonathan's mouth was a thin, grim line and his eyes were bitter with loathing.

"I'll attend to it directly after lunch," he told her savagely.

Cherry cried out hotly, "Jonny, you're going to *pay* her to go away? Gran'sir, isn't that blackmail, and punishable by prison?"

Loyce asked tremulously, "What is this all about?"

Sandra said coolly, "It's about some money Jonny owes me that I've come to collect and don't intend to leave without."

Loyce turned swiftly to Jonathan. "Do you owe her money, Jonny?"

"She thinks so," answered Jonathan wearily. "I told you about it last night, remember? And now it's come to a showdown. She wins, of course. It will be worth it to be quite sure I never set eyes on her again. Go get packed, Sandra, and be ready to leave within an hour."

Highly gratified by the turn of events, Sandra stood up.

"I'll be ready in half an hour," she cooed sweetly. "I'm already packed. In fact, I haven't unpacked."

"That's good," said Cherry, scarlet-cheeked. "Because you're going to be leaving, but you're not taking Jonny's check. Because he's not going to give you one."

"Now, Cherry, wait a minute," Jonathan protested.

"No, *you* wait a minute," Cherry flashed. "I'd have a lot more respect for you if you simply grabbed her by the nape of the neck, slammed her into the car and told her to get going! What kind of man are you, anyway, that you have to pay blackmail to keep from being pursued by a shameless creature like her?"

Loyce was looking from one irate, screaming girl to the other and then at Jonathan; the lovely color had faded from her face, and her eyes were wide with alarm and concern.

Jonathan met Cherry's eyes, and suddenly the tautness went out of his face and he grinned at her. Sandra, seeing the swift exchange of meaningful glances, cried out furiously, "You'd better give me my check, Jonny, or you'll wish you'd never been born."

Jonathan turned to the judge, as though Sandra had not spoken.

"What would you advise, sir, in a case like this?" he asked.

The judge eyed Sandra without warmth.

"Why, I'd simply tell her to get out and stay out, and if she went on with her attempts to harass me, I'd get an injunction against her that would make her 'cease and desist'," he drawled. "She's running a most colossal bluff, my boy. My advice is that you call it here and now, in the presence of witnesses."

Sandra cried out in fury. "Why, you old goat!"

Cherry was on her feet immediately, eyes blazing.

"Don't you swear at Gran'sir," she said hotly, and laid a hand on Sandra's arm. "Come on, you! You're leaving."

Sandra flung Cherry's hand away from her and glared at Jonathan.

"Are you going to listen to that old fool of a judge?" she blazed.

"Since he is a very wise and astute judge and my legal adviser, that's exactly what I'm going to do," Jonathan told her. "I'm thoroughly ashamed that I ever let you bluff me in the first place. But that's all over now. I think you'd better do what Cherry says and get going."

He stood up, caught Sandra's arm

and marched her toward the stairs and up them out of sight.

"Poor Jonny!" said Loyce softly.

"Poor Jonny my eye!" snapped Cherry. "How any man could ever have been taken in by her! Hiding from her, for Pete's sake! Letting her chase him out of his profession! Planning to buy her off with a big fat settlement as if she had really been his wife. Jonny's almost as incredible as she is. I'm not sure I like him any better than I like her. And I purely despise her."

"Oh, now, Cherry you mustn't be hard on the boy," the judge protested. "I'm sure she made things very unpleasant for him."

"Well, what was to stop him from smacking her down?" raged Cherry. "Gran'sir, let's notify him that we'll be needing his room immediately. I've got reservations for the weekend that will fill the place."

"No!" said Loyce so sharply that they both looked at her in swift surprise. Loyce's color deepened and her eyes

153

would not quite meet theirs. "I mean — well, it's not fair to penalize Jonny just because of her behaviour. He's happy here and he's not making any trouble. I think we ought to let him stay until he's ready to go."

Cherry stared at her and then at the judge. For a moment neither spoke, and then Cherry said awkwardly, "Well, of course, honey, if *you* want him to stay — "

"It's not that I want him to stay," Loyce answered uncomfortably. "It's just that I think it would be unfair to make him go just because of Sandra. After all, he wasn't to blame for her coming here. She just hired detectives to trace him and then came. It wasn't really his fault."

"It was, too!" Cherry could not keep back the words. "If he had told her to go chase herself and not encourage her to think he was in love with her, this would never have happened."

"He didn't encourage her to think he was in love with her," Loyce protested

154

so warmly that once more the judge and Cherry exchanged startled, uneasy glances. "If she read more into his intention than was really there — well, after all, a man can't be blamed if a girl convinces herself of something that her common sense tells her isn't true, but that she *wants* to be true so much that she finally makes herself believe it."

The judge and Cherry were staring at Loyce as though they had never set eyes on her before.

"I suppose I'm not making much sense," she managed painfully at last, and there was a pleading in the look she gave them and in the tone of her voice.

"Well, I wouldn't say that," Cherry admitted reluctantly, though it was exactly what she would have said had the speaker been anybody but Loyce. "What doesn't make sense to me is why you're taking up for Jonny. I didn't think you even liked him."

"Well, I *do* like him," Loyce said

awkwardly. "He's kind and he's gentle and he's nice."

She glanced at both of them as though to apologize for the inadequate word.

Upstairs, a door banged sharply open and then Sandra came marching down the stairs, her head held high, her cheeks blazing beneath her deft makeup. She did not glance at the group still about the table in the dining area but marched straight out of the big front door.

Jonathan, his face set and white with anger, came behind her, carrying two large suitcases; and following Jonathan was Eben with two more cases. Elsie brought up the rear. As the men followed Sandra outside, Elsie stopped at the foot of the stairs and watched as the big front door closed behind Eben.

"My sakes alive!" she murmured, and then came to the table. "That was better than a movie. For a minute there I thought she was going to try to kill him. Man, was she ever mad! She called him things I never heard a man say, let alone a woman that's supposed to be a lady."

She looked at the three around the table and saw the forbidding gleam in the judge's eyes and said hastily to Cherry, "He gave her a check."

Cherry cried out angrily. "He *what*?"

Elsie nodded. "He sure did. But I don't reckon it was as big as she was hoping for. She sure screamed some nasty things at him. But she kept the check. He said it was to tide her over until she could get back to work."

"That will do, Elsie!" said the judge sternly.

They had moved into the living room area and Elsie was busy clearing the dining area when Jonathan came back. The sound of Sandra's car was dying away down the drive, and Jonathan paused at the foot of the stairs and faced them, his face taut and drawn.

"There are no apologies I could offer for the outrageous episode that just ended," he said quietly. "I can't begin to tell you how sorry I am or how much I regret it. I'll be packed and away from here as fast as I can."

The judge forestalled Loyce's protest by saying quietly, "You're fed up with the lodge, Jonathan?"

Jonathan looked startled. "You know better than that, sir. It's just that I felt sure you'd want me to leave, after this outrageous affair."

"Oh, Jonny, don't go," stammered Loyce, her voice shaking. "Please don't go!"

Jonathan looked uncertainly at the judge.

"I don't want to go, Loyce, unless I'm no longer welcome here," Jonathan told her. "And that's for you to say, judge. Am I?"

The judge's eyes twinkled beneath his bushy brows, but he answered without a smile, "Loyce is a full partner in the lodge, my boy. She has as much to say about who's to stay as Cherry or I. If she wants you to stay, then you are quite welcome."

Jonathan turned to Cherry, who met his gaze with her chin tilted at a defiant angle and her eyes frosty.

"Cherry?" he asked uncertainly.

"It's up to Loyce," said Cherry coldly. "Personally, I couldn't care less one way or another. And now, if you'll excuse me, I've got work to do."

The door of her small library-office closed behind her, and Jonathan looked gratefully at Loyce and the judge.

"You're all very kind and I'm really very grateful," he said simply.

11

IN the late afternoon, as Loyce came up from the bottom fields, she discovered Jonathan at the stop where the path to the fishing spot joined that to the fields.

She paused for an instant, and color flooded her sun-tanned face as her eyes met his shyly. Then she came on to meet him, eager-eyed and breathless.

"What did you find out, Jonny?" she asked him eagerly.

"It's too soon to have found out anything, Loyce, honey," Jonathan answered her quickly. "I started some inquiries, but it will be several days before we can hope for news. I waited here because I wanted to thank you for taking my part in that ugly mess with Sandra."

"I didn't want you to leave," Loyce told him awkwardly, "until we had found out about Weldon."

Jonathan looked as though she had slapped him. He took a step backward, and his expression hardened.

"Oh, yes, of course. It was your concern for news of Hammett, not any interest in me, that caused you to want me to stay. I was a fool to have thought anything else." His voice was harsh, his eyes bitter.

Loyce put out a hand to touch him, drew it back and locked it tight in her other hand. Her eyes were warm and anxious and her voice was not quite steady when she answered:

"It wasn't altogether that, Jonny. Please believe me. I didn't want you to have to go just because she'd made things so unpleasant for all of us. I didn't feel it was your fault that she followed you around. You seemed happy here, and I didn't see why you couldn't stay on if you wanted to."

Jonathan studied her for a long, tense moment as though not quite sure that he dared believe her. But

161

the earnestness in her eyes, the warm sincerity in her voice dispelled his doubts, and suddenly he smiled warmly at her.

"That's good to know, Loyce. I suppose it *was* my fault, as Cherry pointed out, because I didn't smack her down when the pursuit first started," he admitted ruefully.

"But if Sandra is shameless enough to hire private detectives to trail you, mightn't she do it again when you are somewhere else; when she's spent the money you gave her?"

Jonathan's brows drew together in a small frown. "You know about that?" he asked.

Loyce's color deepened but she managed a faint smile. "Elsie is a terrific tattletale," she reminded him. "And she said the whole thing was better than a movie. Naturally she knew that you gave Sandra a check, and naturally she told us. I'm sorry, Jonny, but there are very few secrets at the lodge."

"I gave her enough to keep her going until she could get back to modeling. Was that wrong, Loyce?"

"Of course not, Jonny," Loyce answered swiftly. "It was kind of you, and I'm awfully glad you did it."

Jonathan's brow cleared. "Well, thanks," he told her. "That's something I hated to have you or Cherry know. Cherry surely made no bones of what she thinks of me for letting myself in for such a messy affair."

"Cherry's young," said Loyce earnestly. "Oh, I know she's only four years younger than I am; but in many ways I'm many years older. To Cherry everything has to be black, very black, or snowy white; there are no in-betweens. But she likes you very much."

"That's nice to know." Jonathan grinned at her and turned to walk with her up the path towards the lodge. At the kitchen steps he asked with a touch of anxiety, "I'll see you at dinner?"

"Oh, yes," she answered.

Emboldened, he asked quickly, "I suppose I couldn't persuade you to go in to town to dinner with me, and maybe a movie afterward, or whatever wild excitement the town affords?"

Loyce looked up at him, bright-eyed and smiling.

"You might try," she suggested gently.

Jonathan's eyes warmed. "Then will you?" he asked.

"Thanks, I'd love to," she answered, and turned toward the steps.

Jonathan laid a swift, restraining hand on her arm, his eyes anxious. "You promise not to stand me up again?" he demanded.

"Oh, Jonny, no. Of course I won't."

For a moment their eyes met and clung, and Jonathan said huskily. "Please don't, Loyce."

There was the faintest possible mist in her eyes, and her smile was tremulous, her voice very low when she said, "I won't, Jonny, ever again."

He stood back then and let her go up the steps and into the house.

In the kitchen, as Loyce flashed through without a word, Elsie and her mother stood staring at each other.

"I reckon you saw what I saw, Muv?" asked Elsie.

"I reckon I did."

"What does it mean, do you reckon?"

"I reckon it means that maybe Loyce has got over that Hammett feller and is getting more than a mite interested in this feller Gayle. And I'm right glad to see it. He seems a likely kind of a feller, even if he does have some right queer lady friends," said Muv. "It's way past time for Loyce to be getting out of them 'down-yonders' she's had since that feller Hammett got killed. Time she was taking a mite of interest in some other man. I'm right surprised, though, that it ain't Hutch."

Elsie shrugged disdainfully. "Oh, who'd bother with Hutch Mayfield when Jonathan Gayle is around? Honest, Muv, he's the most!"

Her mother's eyes twinkled. "Don't you let Jeff hear you saying that," she ordered.

Upstairs, Cherry had just emerged from the shower, a toweling robe tied snugly about her, when Loyce came in, flushed and eager.

"Cherry, Jonny asked me to have dinner with him, and I don't have anything pretty to wear. Lend me something?" she asked.

Cherry's eyes flew wide with surprised pleasure.

"Well, be my guest," she ordered as she swung open the door of her closet.

Loyce was engrossed in the contents of the closet. When she turned she held a copper-colored linen sheath in her hands.

"Would this be all right on me?" she asked hesitantly. "It looks gorgeous on you, but I don't have your vivid coloring."

"Stop low-rating yourself or I'll smack you," Cherry ordered her sternly.

"That will be wonderful on you. Let me fix your hair. You just brush it back and wind it in a knot so tight you can hardly blink, and it's a shame. It's such a beautiful color, like the inside of a chestnut burr."

"You're the one with the lovely hair, Cherry," said Loyce humbly.

"Phooey!" Cherry protested inelegantly. "I'm the one that was called carrot-top when we were growing up, remember?"

Later, when Loyce and Jonathan had departed, Cherry stared for a long moment at the door that had closed behind them. The judge watched Cherry and waited.

"Well," she said at last, and turned to face him. "What do you think, Gran'sir?"

"That they make a very handsome couple," he answered.

"Oh, they do that, they do indeed," Cherry agreed, but it was obvious she was thinking of something else.

"Do you mind, honey?" asked the judge after a long silent moment.

Cherry looked sharply at him, frowning.

"Mind? I'm tickled pink; aren't you? I mean I'm tickled to see Loyce interested in pretty clothes and men again," she answered.

"I wondered if you minded that the man is Jonathan." The judge's tone was grave.

"Oh, well, I think she could do a lot better for herself," Cherry admitted. "Jonny seems to me a pretty weak character. Any man who'd let himself be hounded by a dame like that Elliott creature — "

"That's something you don't understand, honey."

"Well, I don't suppose I do. And, frankly, Gran'sir, I couldn't care less," Cherry stated flatly. "It's just that if Loyce *is* coming back to life again, I can't help wishing it could be with somebody with a little more sense than to step into a woman-trap baited by a gal like Sandra Elliott."

"It's not that you want Jonny for

168

yourself?" asked the judge.

"For Pete's sake, I do not," Cherry protested warmly. "Oh, he's nice and a novelty; Loyce and I have never known a man like him before. And somehow I feel maybe that's just as well. Can you imagine Job letting a woman crowd him into a corner and try to marry him against his wishes and finally demand to be paid off?"

The judge hesitated for a moment and then said frankly, "Look, honey, you know my attitude toward gossip. But there is something I feel that you should know. That is, if you have decided to marry Job."

Puzzled, Cherry answered, "Well, he wants me to, and I'm very fond of him. What's up, Gran'sir?"

"It's just that a very persistent rumor is going around that the Widow Marshall is tired of being a widow and that she and Job are seeing quite a bit of each other," the judge told her.

"You mean Betty Marshall's after

Job?" demanded Cherry hotly.

"So rumor has it."

"Well, well, *well*," murmured Cherry softly, and her eyes narrowed.

The judge watched her for a moment, and when she seemed disinclined to speak, he said quietly, "A woman like Betty Marshall can be very dangerous, honey."

"Dangerous?" Cherry repeated in a tone of amused disdain. "Why, she's just a kid, Gran'sir."

"She's a young and very attractive widow, and she's obviously tired of living at home with her family and would like a home of her own, *and* a husband."

"And Job would give her a nice home and be a very good husband," Cherry admitted slowly. "Is that what you're telling me, Gran'sir?"

"I don't usually interfere in your affairs or Loyce's," the judge reminded her. "But I don't like just sitting here helpless and watching you throw away something you may one day wake up and find that you really wanted very much."

Cherry was alarmed and unable to conceal it.

"What do you think I should do, Gran'sir?" she asked as humbly as she had asked the same question when she had been a child.

"I think you should make up your mind once and for all whether or not you are in love with Job," he told her firmly. "If you are not, then set him free to make a life of his own. If you are, then make up your mind if you want to marry him. It's as simple as that, honey."

"Well, yes, I suppose it is," Cherry said unhappily.

"But you must be very sure, honey. Marriage is a long-term contract, and there are no options. And I strongly disapprove of divorce," the judge told her firmly. "I just thought you ought to know about Betty's pursuit of Job. In fact, it could easily be, since she is young and very pretty and a fine little housekeeper, that Job is pursuing her."

"It could be, at that," Cherry said ruefully.

The judge watched her and waited, and at last she said uncomfortably, "Honestly, Gran'sir, I'm not quite sure whether I want to marry Job or not. Oh, I'm very fond of him and we have fun together and all that. But is that being in love, enough love to get married on?"

The judge grinned at her like an impish small boy.

"It's been a great many years since I was qualified to answer that, honey," he pointed out. "Maybe you'd better just ask your heart, honey, and follow whatever it tells you to do."

The judge waited and watched her as she scowled thoughtfully.

"I'll give it some thought," she said at last.

"You do that, honey," said the judge.

Cherry nodded and bent to kiss him good night. But instead of going up to her room she went out on the wide verandah to the big swing that hung behind the curtain of vines at the end of the porch. She curled up in the swing and looked out over the sweep of mountains, and her thoughts were busy with Job and Betty Marshall.

She was still in the swing when Jonathan and Loyce came back. She stayed where she was, unwilling to intrude on their good nights. They paused on the steps, and Loyce turned and looked out over the starlit scene and drew a deep, unsteady breath.

"Oh, it's been such a lovely evening." She sighed. "I feel as if I'd just started living again. If only we find out — "

"We'll find out that Weldon was on that plane and that you've been torturing yourself for nothing," Jonathan told her, sharpness in his voice. "You are the loveliest girl he could ever have hoped to meet, and he would never have run out on you. That's something you have to get out of your mind here and now, because it's what we will learn when my friends have been able to answer the wires I've sent."

"I hope so, Jonny. Oh, I do hope so," said Loyce softly, her voice slightly shaken.

"Well, we will," said Jonathan, and held open the door for her. "I'm just as sure of it as if I had seen him board the plane myself."

12

IT was two days later that Jonathan asked to ride into town with Cherry when she went in for the mail and the marketing. She was glad of his company and chattered gaily as they drove the few miles to town. In fact, her chatter was so gay that Jonathan studied her curiously and broke in to say, amused, "I'm not quite sure if all this light chitchat is because you despise me and would like me to get going."

Cherry stared at him in surprise.

"How could I possibly despise you after all you've done for Loyce?" she protested.

Jonathan scowled at her. "What have I done for Loyce?" he wanted to know.

Cherry flushed but gave her attention to driving. After a moment she confessed,

"I'm a stinker, Jonny. I was on the verandah when you brought her home from dinner in town night before last. And I heard enough to make me believe that you'd found out what was worrying her so terribly and were clearing it up for her. I didn't mean to eavesdrop, Jonny, truly, but I may as well admit I'm glad I did. I've been so worried about her."

Jonathan scowled straight ahead for a long moment, and they were just entering the limits of the small town when he said quietly, "I can't tell you anything about it, Cherry, except that she had been terribly depressed about this Hammett fellow."

"She believes he wasn't on the plane and just used the crash as a means of running out on her," Cherry interrupted. "That's it, isn't it?"

"And you don't believe it?"

"Good grief — no!" Cherry exploded. "Nobody could who had ever seen them together. Why, he was completely insane about her. If she so much as left the room, he wandered around like a lost soul until she came back. How could she possibly believe that he wasn't deeply in love with her?"

"She has a very deep-rooted inferiority complex, and it's been giving her a very bad time ever since the plane crash," Jonathan said quietly.

"But aren't there ways of proving whether or not he was on the plane?" demanded Cherry. "And if he wasn't, then where is he? He couldn't just vanish into thin air; he was a fairly important member of the British Embassy staff."

"I'm having private detectives and a friend who is in the newspaper business check all angles," Jonathan told her. "That's why I was eager to get into town today; not to pick up mail but to make a few long distance telephone calls. If you'll drop me off at the telephone exchange and pick me up there when you're ready to go back to the lodge, I'll see what my friend and the detectives have found out."

"So Loyce got the idea about private detectives from Sandra," Cherry said, as she slowed the car for a traffic light.

"It would seem so."

Cherry nodded thoughtfully. "Then I'm glad you gave Sandra a check. I'd send her one if I knew where she was."

"Oh, Sandra will be all right," said Jonathan, and now his tone was grim. "There's the exchange just ahead. I'll be ready to go back when you are. And thanks for the lift."

"Thanks for the lift you've given Loyce!" said Cherry, and beamed warmly at him as he got out of the car and crossed the sidewalk.

She turned and drove back to the town's proudest possession, a big supermarket. There was an enormous parking lot, and as she parked her car and locked it, a group came out of the market and walked toward a battered but dependable-looking car.

Cherry was so absorbed in her

thoughts that she all but ran into the girl who had suddenly stopped directly in her path.

"Hello, Cherry," said Betty Marshall. Betty's golden head was bare, and the sunlight glinted lovingly on its golden waves, held in place by a narrow blue ribbon. Her gingham dress was blue and white-checked and had been washed until it had faded and was shrunken. On her feet she wore canvas sneakers and no hose. And yet Cherry had to admit that Betty was lovely.

In spite of herself, Cherry felt her spirits droop slightly as she chatted for a moment with the girl and fought hard to keep Job's name from her lips. Betty's father, a tall, lean, raw-boned man, hailed the girl sharply, and she smiled wistfully at Cherry and ran to crowd herself into the old car among the half-dozen children ranging in ages from five to six up to ten or twelve. There was scarcely room in the car for all of them and as Cherry watched Betty force her way into the back of the car and heard the children screaming at her and pushing her, Cherry was deeply sorry for Betty. No wonder Betty wanted to marry Job or anybody who would take her out of the overcrowded home in which she was no longer welcome.

She forced a chuckle as she selected a marketing cart and started filling the list Muv had given her.

"Us Brambletts," she mocked herself ruefully, "surely take a heap of convincing from our men folks."

She hoped vainly for a glimpse of Job as she finished her errands and drove back to the telephone exchange to pick up Jonathan, who was waiting for her with a smile that lifted her heart. For it told her that his friends had been able to give him news that would banish Loyce's grief and depression.

"Is it all right, Jonny?" she asked anxiously.

"He was aboard the plane. There is no doubt of that," he told her.

"Oh, Jonny, let's hurry back and tell

180

her." Cherry breathed, and looked up at him in eager warmth and happiness.

Back at the lodge, Elsie and Eben came out to help unload the marketing, and Jonathan asked, "Where is Miss Loyce?"

"Oh, she's down at the barn looking after that new batch of pheasants that just hatched out," Eben answered. Jonathan nodded and hurried around the house and down toward the barn.

Loyce was just emerging from the pheasants' cage when she saw Jonathan. Hastily she locked the door and came swiftly to meet him.

"Come along," said Jonathan, and took her hand and drew her with him down the trail to the place where they had had lunch that day that now seemed a century before.

Loyce looked anxiously at him, and something in his face gave away the news he had to tell her. Her heart sang a small, frightened song as they reached the spot and he drew a thick envelope from his pocket.

"There is not the faintest doubt that Weldon Hammett was aboard that plane when it crashed," he told her gravely. "He did not run out on you and you should be ashamed that you ever thought he would."

He placed the envelope in her hands, and she dropped down on the large flat rock where they had had their lunch and held the envelope with hands that shook as tears slid down her face.

"Oh, my darling," she whispered so softly that the words barely reached Jonathan. Knowing they were not meant for him, he walked away from her, leaving her alone in that moment of healing peace.

She wept there as she had not wept since the news of the crash. They were tears that came from her heart, but they came, too, from wounded pride and self-respect that beneath the healing tears grew sound and free again.

When at last Jonathan came back to her, she sat with the sheets of paper in her hands and looked up at him with eyes washed clean of tears. And on her face there was a radiance that seemed to bathe Jonathan in it's lovely glow.

"I don't know how I'll ever thank you, Jonny," she said softly, her voice husky with tears.

Jonathan looked down at her where she sat on the big rock, her face lifted, her eyes soft and warm despite the recent tears. And there was that in his eyes that made her catch her breath on a small, startled gasp. And then Jonathan smiled at her.

"Oh, we'll think of something one of these days," he told her, and his tone made the words a promise that brought a soft touch of carnation-pink to her tear-streaked face.

His tone, the look in his eyes, brought her back to an awareness of her recent tears, and she got to her feet with a touch of endearing awkwardness of a child.

"I must look a sight," she stammered. "I don't weep prettily. I get all bleary-eyed and red-nosed and ugly."

"Loyce," Jonathan's voice was stern, as his hands caught her by the shoulders and gave her a shake, "you are never, so long as you live, going to say or even think anything like that about yourself. Do you understand?"

"Well, I just meant that no woman looks attractive when she's crying," she stammered.

"You couldn't look ugly if you tried," Jonathan told her swiftly. "Not to me, anyway. You are lovely and sweet and kind, and I'll tell you more about how I fell toward you later on. For now it's enough for me to say that I never want to hear you tear yourself down. You've got to believe that you are radiantly lovely; it shouldn't be hard for you to do. You *do* have a mirror, don't you?"

She managed a soft, breathless laugh.

"Well, of course I do," she responded. "But I also have a radiantly lovely young sister, remember?"

"And all your life you've been jealous of her," Jonathan stated so flatly that for a moment she could only blink at him, not at all sure she had heard him correctly.

"Why, that's not true!" she gasped, outraged. "I adore her."

"Sure you do," Jonathan answered. "But all your life you've felt that she was prettier and more attractive than you; you've let yourself develop a perfectly insane and wicked inferiority complex that has made you try to withdraw from the whole human race. And when Weldon fell in love with you, you were so unsure of yourself that you were sure it couldn't possibly last — that he would tire of you, because you were unsophisticated. Apparently it never occurred to you that your very difference from the women he had known was a great part of your charm. You should be ashamed of yourself, Loyce, not only for doubting him, but for doubting your own charms."

"I'm ashamed of doubting him," Loyce said shakily. "But I never thought I had any charms."

Jonathan's gesture was one of exasperation.

"I don't know what I'm going to do with you." He sighed.

Color flashed in her cheeks and for a moment there was a spark in her eyes.

"Well, you *could* just let me alone," she flashed.

"That's the one thing I'm not going to do," Jonathan assured her firmly.

Anger now was burning within her, anger that momentarily drowned out her gratitude.

"And just what makes you think you have anything to do with what happens to me from here on out?" she demanded hotly.

Jonathan studied her for a moment and then gave her a disarming grin.

"I've met Hutchens Mayfield," he told her, as though no further explanation could possibly be necessary.

Loyce caught her breath. "So?" she snapped. "He's a very fine man."

"Sure he is," Jonathan answered,

"and full of ambition."

"Well, is there anything wrong about that?" she demanded.

"Not a bit. More power to him. If I stay here long enough, I'll even vote for him some day," Jonathan answered. "He's a fine man, but he's not the man for you."

"Well, for heaven's sake!" Loyce gasped faintly.

Jonathan grinned at her. "I'm not going to tell you *now* that I'm in love with you. But if you're as smart as I think you are, you must have guessed it."

"How could I?" she stammered. "This is perfectly crazy! I won't listen to any more."

"There isn't going to be any more — now," Jonathan told her . "We've got the rest of the summer. I'm not going anywhere, and you live here, so we'll have plenty of time. But make no mistake about it, Loyce. You're my girl, and before the summer is over you're going to admit it."

His hands still held her by the shoulders and he was looking down at her with his heart in his eyes. Loyce met his gaze, and as he watched he saw her eyes widen slightly. Beneath his hands he felt the small, slight tremor that spread through her body.

"Loyce, are you afraid of me?" he demanded sharply.

"Why, of course not! What a silly question!" she stammered. "It's just that everything is happening so fast! I'm confused."

Jonathan's hands dropped and he took a backward step away from her. As though he no longer trusted them, he jammed his hands into his pockets.

"So be it," he said grimly. "So you're confused. Well, I've never been noted for patience, but I can wait for you to get yourself straightened out mentally. I know you've been under a terrific strain since the crash. Shall I go away?"

She caught her breath, and alarm rather than fear was in her eyes now.

"Go away? Oh, no, Jonny!" she

cried, and hot color burned in her face and her eyes dropped away from his. "I mean — I wouldn't want you to go, unless you wanted to."

"You know darned well I don't," he told her. "But if you are going to be afraid of me every time I mention the fact that I love you, then I'd better go now, while there is still some very faint chance that I can get you out of my heart."

"Oh, Jonny," she whispered faintly. "Just let me have a little while to adjust."

"To what? Hammett's been dead more than a year," Jonathan pointed out with brutal frankness.

She cringed slightly. "I know," she said huskily. "I have adjusted to it. But it's only been a few minutes since I became sure that he didn't just run out on me. I have to get used to that!"

He studied her for a moment, and then he drew a deep breath and lifted his shoulders in a slight gesture that was not quite a shrug.

"And how long will that take? Months? Years perhaps?"

"Oh, no, Jonny, no!"

He nodded at the stricken look in her eyes, the tone of her voice.

"I'll stick around for a while then," he told her harshly. "And when and if the time comes that you're willing to face up to the fact that I love you and want to marry you, maybe you'll let me know."

And without waiting for her answer, he turned and strode off down the trail toward the falls.

13

SUMMER had come to the mountains, and with it the onrush of tourists from the low country, fleeing from the heat of city sidewalks and tall buildings. With the coming of the tourist the tempo of life at the county seat had been speeded up. The tourists had to be entertained — and their entertainment had to be quite different from anything they were accustomed to at home. Thus, there were taffy-pulls, fish-fries, square dances and picnics.

The lodge was overflowing with fishing guests. Cherry was so busy that she scarcely realized the change in Loyce until one night, the first in a week or more, when there were only the two girls, the judge and Jonathan at dinner. She looked across the table and saw Loyce was flushed and bright-eyed and pretty. She noticed the look in Jonathan's eyes and barely restrained a faint whistle of surprise.

"There's going to be a shindig down at Joe Mason's barn tonight," Cherry announced. "Job's coming for me. Wouldn't you like to go, Loyce? It would do you good."

Loyce looked up and met Jonathan's eyes, and his own widened with surprise and delight.

"Would you like to go, Jonny?" she asked.

Jonathan held himself sternly in check, unwilling to allow a hope that had been smacked down so often to rear its head again.

"I'm the city slicker myself," he pointed out. "I'm afraid I wouldn't know what a 'shindig' is. Sounds like fun, though."

"Oh, it's mountain name for square dancing," Cherry explained gaily even as she covertly watched the two. "A barn dance. You've never heard such music and may never again, unless it's in another mountain community. But it is fun. Loyce is a marvellous square dancer."

"I'm not, really," Loyce began, and caught her breath beneath the look in Jonathan's eyes. "Well, maybe I am, if Cherry says I am. Cherry's the expert in the family."

"Well, I'm the fellow with two left feet and a tin ear when it comes to square dancing," Jonathan said, and smiled warmly at Loyce. "But I'm supposed to be a fast study. Maybe you could teach me. That is, if you wouldn't mind?"

"I wouldn't mind at all," Loyce assured him radiantly, and for just an instant Cherry exchanged startled glances with the judge, who was also watching Loyce and Jonathan.

Later, upstairs, Loyce asked Cherry, "I haven't been to a barn dance in so long, Cherry. Do I have anything suitable to wear?"

"Well, of course," said Cherry judiciously, her eyes merry, "you really should have something simple but exquisite in gold lamé or black velvet, with a yard or so of pearls — you zany! Anything suitable for a barn dance! There's just one thing in your wardrobe I forbid you to wear, and that's your overalls. Them's for daytime, not for dances."

Loyce laughed joyously and it was such a lovely sound and so unusual that Cherry blinked in surprised delight as Loyce danced off to get dressed.

Downstairs, waiting for Job, Cherry perched on the arm of a chair across from the judge and asked curiously, "What do you think, Gran'sir?"

"About what, chick?"

"Now don't be coy with me, Gran'sir!" Cherry protested. "What do you think about Loyce and Jonny?"

"I think they make a very handsome couple, and they seem to be discovering that fact," the judge answered. "Do you mind?"

"Mind? You asked me that ages ago because you had some crazy idea that

194

I wanted Jonny for myself. But how could I, when I've got Job?"

"Oh?" The judge's eyebrows went up slightly. "*Have* you?"

"That," Cherry told him firmly, "is what I propose to find out tonight."

"Oh, then you've made up your mind?" asked the judge.

Cherry chuckled like an amused child.

"Do you know something, Gran'sir? I don't think there's ever been the faintest doubt in my mind about that," she admitted frankly. "I just had to have a good hard jolt to wake me up to the truth."

"And the fact that Betty was after Job was the jolt?" asked the judge.

Cherry nodded soberly. "I'm terribly sorry for Betty; she's had a rough deal. But I'm not sorry enough to give her my Job."

The judge eyed her curiously for a moment.

"So you aren't going to give her Job?" he repeated.

"I certainly am not!"

"Well, *could* you, if you wanted to?"

Puzzled, Cherry stared at him, frowning.

"And what's that supposed to mean, Gran'sir?" she asked him cautiously.

"Only that it always puzzles me how women can feel they can hand a man over as if they'd bought and paid for him and were taking him back to the exchange desk."

Cherry colored faintly.

"Did I sound like that about Job, Gran'sir?" she asked humbly. "I didn't mean to. What I meant was that if Betty wants him, I'll fight her for him; but if Job wants her instead of me, I'll be a lady about it if it kills me, even if I have to go into a decline and be a permanent old maid."

"Who's going to be an old maid?" demanded Job as he swung open the door and came into the house.

Cherry jumped and flushed scarlet as she scowled at him.

"Job Tallent, how long have you been standing there eavesdropping?" she demanded.

"I wasn't eavesdropping," Job protested with some heat. "I just opened the door, and somebody said something about being a permanent old maid, and my curiosity was aroused. That's all. Shall I go back outside and ring? I thought you'd hear the car and be warned I was approaching."

Cherry smiled warmly at him and bent to kiss her grandfather's cheek just as Jonathan and Loyce came down the stairs. Loyce wore a wide-skirted cotton print dress that hugged her upper body and spilled out into many gores below the narrow waist.

"Hi, you two, are you going to the shindig?" Job demanded.

"In my car, Job honey, so don't worry," Loyce told him. "Is that all right with you? Cherry invited us."

"Well, of course," Job answered. "I just didn't know that you cared about barn dances, Loyce. It's been much too long since you've been to one. You'll be the belle of the ball."

Loyce swept Jonathan out of the house, the bright scarf of her laughter floating back to them as they exchanged swift glances.

Job whistled softly and looked at Cherry with raised brows. "That really *was* Loyce, wasn't it?" he asked.

"Or reasonable facsimile." Cherry laughed. "Oh, Job, isn't it wonderful? She's beginning to live again."

"Well, hooray for her!" said Job with deep sincerity. "Well, shall we get going?"

They said good night to the judge and went out to where Job's car was waiting. Job seated Cherry and slid behind the wheel, and as the car rolled down the drive, picking up speed as it neared the county road, Cherry glanced at him in the dim light from the instrument panel.

"I suppose Betty will be there?" she asked sweetly.

"Betty?" Job glanced at her and back

at the road as he negotiated the turn. "Betty who?"

"Oh, now, Job, *please*!"

"I suppose you mean Betty Marshall." Job's tone was a trifle stiff.

"Well, who else would I mean?"

"I'm afraid I wouldn't know," Job said, and then his tone sharpened. "I can't understand why all you girls have your knives out for that girl. She's a decent, honest, straightforward girl, and she's had a very rough deal."

"Do tell!" Cherry murmured dryly, but her hands were clenched tightly in her lap.

"Well, it's true," said Job harshly. "It can't be much fun for her living there with that old sourpuss of a father and that stepmother with her own brood of youngsters, resenting every bite Betty eats and working her half to death. And Betty can't get a job and leave them, because she has no training that would make it possible for her to earn enough to live on. But to hear the girls around town talk, you'd think Betty was a siren out of an old movie."

"Well, simmer down, pal, simmer down," Cherry said. "I only asked if she would be at the dance. I know you've been seeing a lot of her, and I thought you would probably know."

Job drew the car to a halt beside the road, well over on the edge, and turned to her with an air of a man who had something on his mind.

"I haven't been seeing a lot of Betty, as you express it," he stated flatly. "I took her to a box supper at the church one night when you were all tied up at the lodge with a houseful of fishing guests. I've seen her a few times on the street; we went to a movie one night because I felt sorry for her. I would have told you about it."

"Well, I'm sorry for Betty, too," Cherry managed after a moment, her voice shaking slightly, "but not sorry enough to let her marry you. Because that's what I'm going to do, and it's illegal for a man to have two wives."

There was a stunned moment before

Job could convince himself that he had really heard what he had wanted so long to hear.

"What did you say?" he asked at last, his own voice far from steady.

"I said that I wanted to marry you, Job; that is, if you still want me to," Cherry managed shakily.

"If I still want you to!" Job said barely above his breath. His arms reached for her and drew her close and hard against him, and his lips sought and found her own in a kiss that seemed to close like warm, gentle fingers about her heart and lift it to her lips for his taking.

There was an interval that might have been minutes or only seconds while they savored to the full the perfection of that exquisite time. Then Job lifted his head and put her a few inches away from him, and in the dim light from the instrument panel she saw that his face was twisted by a puzzled scowl.

"Is this on the level, Cherry?" he asked her huskily. "You're not just taking me for a ride? You mean it? You want to marry me?"

Quick tears sprang to Cherry's eyes at the aching humility in his voice, and she framed her face between her two palms and raised her own face to set her mouth against his.

"Oh, darling, yes, with all my heart," she whispered when her lips were free for speech. "And I'm a low-down so-and-so to have taken so long to know the truth. You'll despise me."

"Now, that I doubt."

"You will when I tell you that it was jealousy of Betty that made me realize I loved you. Isn't that a terrible confession? Now do you despise me?"

Job laughed and his arms tightened about her.

"You want to know something?" he told her confidentially. "I've been in love with you since we went to school together. But I wasn't in any great hurry for us to be married until Gayle showed up at the lodge. And then I knew that if you didn't marry me, I'd have a very lonely old age; because there couldn't be anybody else for me but you."

"Not even Betty?" she teased.

"Not anybody," Job assured her firmly.

"Poor Betty!" said Cherry later as they finally remembered the dance and Job drove on.

"Don't make fun of her, Cherry," said Job sharply.

"Darling!" Cherry was hurt that he should misunderstand. "How could I? I was just thinking. Do you suppose she'd like to come and live at the lodge? She would be very useful, and we could pay her enough for spending money, and she'd have no expenses. Do you think she'd like that?"

"I think she'd love it, and I love you for thinking of it," Job told her. "It adds one more to the several million reasons I love you, come to think of it."

Ahead of them a wide sweep of driveway opened up, and at the end of it the Mason barn, a huge square building with a few windows here and there, blazed with yellow light.

As Job parked the car beside the drive, thrusting its nose between those of cars of all vintages and makes, he looked down at Cherry.

"I suppose we'll have to go in?" he asked reluctantly.

"I'm afraid so," Cherry sounded equally reluctant, and then she asked lightly. "Will your boss object to your living at the lodge instead of at your station?"

Job frowned in bewilderment.

"What a silly question! We'll be living at the station, of course; where else? It's my job, honey, and I wouldn't want any other."

Cherry sat erect. "Oh, but, Job, I can't go away and leave Gran'sir," she protested.

"Now look, Cherry, we're going to be married and of course you are coming to live at the station," he told her sternly. "Mother has been wanting to go to Florida and live with my sister and that will leave the house for you to boss single-handed. Don't tell me you won't live there. Cherry, it's a beautiful place! You'll love it!"

"Oh, I'm sure I will, darling. Any place where you are will be a beautiful place to me," Cherry assured him, and was suitably rewarded. "It's just that I hate to leave Gran'sir. Still, Loyce will be there, and I can train Betty to take over my job."

Job said quietly, "For a moment you had me worried."

Cherry look up at him in swift compunction.

"Did I, darling? I'm sorry. Forgive me?"

Cherry framed his face between her two hands and set her mouth on his in a kiss of lingering tenderness.

When at last they left the car and walked toward the barn, they were hand in hand. Just before they reached the entrance — double doors large enough to permit a two-horse team to enter — Loyce and Jonathan came to greet them.

"Where have you been?" Loyce asked. "I was worried about you, afraid you'd had an accident."

Cherry looked up at Job, and her smile was a lovely thing to see.

"Shall we tell her?" she asked lightly.

"Why not? I'll climb up on the roof and broadcast it to the world if you like," Job answered with an expansive grin.

"We've been getting ourselves engaged," beamed Cherry.

She was so absorbed, so wrapped in her own happiness that she did not catch the swift flicker that crossed Loyce's face — an expression of dismay that was swallowed up almost immediately by Loyce's protestations of delight and congratulations. But Jonathan, who had been watching Loyce, saw that swift flicker of dismay, and for a moment his jaw hardened and his eyes were bleak.

Cherry, bubbling with happiness, said

eagerly, "You boys trot along inside. I want to talk to Loyce a minute."

Job chuckled. "Might as well start learning to obey orders, I suppose. She's a very managing female. Come on, Gayle. Let's see if we can find ourselves partners for the next hoe-down."

When they were alone, Cherry drew Loyce to a spot near a big oak tree that shaded the corner of the barn and said eagerly, "Job says we'll have to live at the ranger station. But I had an idea coming down. What would you think of asking Betty Marshall to come and live at the lodge? I could teach her how to handle reservations and the books and all. And of course, you'll be there."

The shadows beneath the oak, newly leaved and rustling slightly in the crisp air, concealed Loyce's face from her, and Loyce's voice was quite steady as she answered, "Yes, of course I'll be there."

"Betty is having a rotten time of it

207

at home and she hasn't any business training. But I remember she was a whiz at arithmetic in school, so she won't have any trouble with the bookkeeping, I know." Cherry rushed on. "And she'll be company for you and Gran'sir. What do you think?"

Loyce said quietly, "I think it's a wonderful idea. Betty's here tonight. Why don't you talk to her and see what she thinks."

"You don't think I ought to talk to Gran'sir first?" asked Cherry.

"I am sure he will be perfectly agreeable. Betty's a nice girl and a very deserving one. She would get along beautifully with the Mitchells. If Betty would like to come to the lodge and take over for you, I think it would be a wonderful arrangement," said Loyce and her voice was completely steady. "I'm so happy for you and Job, Cherry. You've known each other so long, it couldn't be anything but a perfect marriage."

"You're sweet, Loyce. And I hope

some day — " Cherry broke off awkwardly and added, "We'd better get into the dancing and protect our men folks from predatory females. I don't trust these tourist gals worth a cent."

Loyce managed a smile and walked, head up, eyes straight ahead, back into the big, noisy barn.

14

WHEN the dance was over and Jonathan and Loyce were driving back to the lodge, she sat very quietly beside him.

Jonathan tried tentatively to talk to her about the dance, the weird but somehow toe-tickling music. She answered in monosyllables, and when at last he parked the car beside the lodge he turned swiftly to her and stopped her as she started to climb out.

"So Cherry and Job are getting married," he said. "You'll miss her when she goes away."

"Yes, of course. But I'll keep very busy." Her voice stumbled and broke.

"And what happens when you get married and go away?" asked Jonathan.

"Oh, I won't," Loyce answered hurriedly, and fought the break in her voice. "We can't both leave Gran'sir, after all he's done for us."

"I rather imagined that would be the way you would feel," said Jonathan grimly. "The born martyr!"

"I'm not!" she flashed at him hotly.

"Then I've been a fool to think for so much as a moment that you could ever learn to love me." Jonathan's voice was harsh.

"That's not true, darling." She threw aside all pretense and faced him in the dim light that felt its way through the tall trees. "I do love you. I adore you. But you *do* understand that both Cherry and I cannot abandon Gran'sir. Don't you see that?"

"I see that you, being you, would feel that way."

"Well, what other way can I feel?" she burst out. Now there were tears sliding down her cheeks, but she was unaware of them until she felt their salt on her lips. "He brought us here when we were only babies. He's brought us up and loved us and cared for us; and now he's old and crippled. How can you possibly think we would both go off and leave him now?"

There was a moment of silence, and then she asked huskily, "I don't suppose you'd be willing to live here permanently if we were married?"

"Of course not," Jonathan answered violently.

"Of course not," she echoed forlornly.

"See here, Loyce, I can't just sit around a place like this the rest of my life," he told her sharply. "After all, I put in a good many years learning my profession. Naturally I want to go back to it; and naturally, I want to take you with me as my wife."

"Naturally," she whispered miserably. "And naturally I can't abandon Gran'sir. So that leaves us very little to say except good-bye."

"Apparently," said Jonathan grimly, and got out of the car. "I'll get my stuff together tomorrow and take off. I've hung around here long enough waiting for you to get over eating your heart out about that Hammett fellow. I'm not going to hang around here waiting for you to get rid of that martyr complex that took over when the inferiority gave up."

"I'm sorry, Jonny," she whispered forlornly, and brushed past him up the steps and into the house.

When Jonathan came down to breakfast the next morning Loyce had already vanished. Cherry was waiting for him, radiant and excited.

"I talked to Gran'sir at breakfast about having Betty Marshall up here to train her for my work," she reported gaily. "Betty was so tickled the poor girl nearly fainted; and Gran'sir thought it was a marvellous idea. I think he's so tickled that I've finally made up my mind about Job that he'd have accepted 'most anybody I wanted to bring in."

She poured a fresh cup of coffee for him and leaned her elbow on the table and rested her chin on her palm, her eyes brimming with merriment.

"You want to know something funny?" she asked.

"I can't think of anything I'd like better than to hear something funny."

"Gran'sir thought I was in danger of falling in love with you." Cherry's tone invited him to laugh, but instead Jonathan merely looked at her in complete stupefaction.

"He couldn't possibly have," he protested.

"Oh, but he did!" Cherry bubbled with laughter, and sobered as she added hastily, "Oh, if it hadn't been for Job, I would have, Jonny. You're a grand person and I am tremendously fond of you. But of course with me it's always been Job, though it took me quite a spell to discover it."

She chuckled and offered more coffee, but Jonathan refused.

"Where is His Honor? Available for a chat? I want to say good-bye," Jonathan told her as he stood up.

"Good-bye?" Cherry repeated, wide-eyed. "Oh, Jonny, you're not leaving now. You've got to stay for my wedding!"

"Thanks, Cherry, that's sweet of you, but I've loafed long enough," Jonathan told her. "Way past time I was getting back among the torts and briefs, or I'll have to learn the language all over again."

Cherry asked quietly, "Have you and Loyce quarreled?"

Jonathan caught his breath. "Now that's a silly question." His tone was harsh.

"Look, can't you realize, Cherry, that I'm a city slicker? I can take just so much of this mountain stuff."

"Well, yes, of course, Jonny, if you say so." Cherry was very much subdued and understandably puzzled. "Gran'sir is out on the side verandah."

"Thanks," said Jonathan curtly, and marched out.

The judge dropped his newspaper as Jonathan came out and smiled a warm, friendly smile of greeting, and motioned to a chair beside him, commenting pleasantly on the perfection of the morning.

"I thought I'd take off, Judge," Jonathan told him when the first greetings were over. "Loafing gets to be a chore after a while, and I've been down here for weeks."

"It's been a real pleasure to have you, Jonny, and I'll hate seeing you go," said the judge quietly.

"Thank you, sir," Jonathan answered. "it's been pretty wonderful here and I hope I may come back some time for another vacation. But of course I'm going to be pretty busy for the next few years getting a practice established."

The judge smiled. "I take it you are no longer disillusioned with the law?"

Jonathan managed an answering grin. "Only with some of those who practice it."

"Oh, well, there are crooks and scoundrels in all trades, and we just have to learn to live with that fact," the judge answered.

For a moment the two men sat in a rather awkward silence. There was much each wanted to say to the other,

216

and yet it was difficult to bring the subject to the fore.

"When you first came Loyce was living in a tight little world all her own, locked up in some bitterness that I could not feel was entirely due to her grief for Weldon, although I knew that hit her hard," said the judge slowly, his eyes on the scene before them, dappled with sunshine and shadow, the garden agleam with summer beauty. "I don't know what miracle you worked, but I'm very grateful for it. In the past few weeks she has come out of the shadows and has become the girl she was before Weldon came. I'm very fond of my granddaughters, Jonny."

"You have every reason to be, sir," said Jonathan. "They are fine girls and very beautiful."

"More than anything in the world, I want their happiness," said the judge slowly. "Even if it takes them away from me to a place where I see them only rarely, I want them to be happy."

Jonathan's eyes dropped to his hands,

locked and hanging between his knees.

"Cherry will be in and out of the lodge every few days," he pointed out. "And Loyce will be here permanently."

"I hope not," said the judge quietly.

Jonathan looked up at him swiftly.

"I mean I hope Loyce will find a husband and go away to a home of her own some day," said the judge, and looked straight at Jonathan.

For a moment the eyes of the two men locked and held. And it was Jonathan who spoke, saying something he had had no intention of saying. "Now that Cherry is getting married and leaving the lodge, I'm quite sure that Loyce has no intention of marrying."

"She told you that?" probed the judge.

"She told me that," he admitted, and then was appalled at the realization of his betrayal. "I mean sir, that she told me — that is, I'm sure she feels that she and Cherry can't both desert you."

The judge nodded, smiled faintly but with a touch of triumph in his eyes.

"So I was right," he said. "You *are* in love with Loyce and she is in love with you. So what's the problem?"

"I'm sorry, sir, but I'm afraid that's something you will have to ask Loyce," Jonathan replied stiffly.

"And don't think I won't!" said the judge. "That's exactly what I'll do. You won't be leaving today, son. As a personal favor to me, stay over until tomorrow, will you? You can get a better train that way — if you insist on going, that is. Cherry has to meet a couple of fellows who didn't want to drive up; she can take you to the station when she goes to collect them."

Jonathan hesitated.

"I'll be glad to wait over another day, judge," he said at last.

"Good! Then you'd better run along and get in a final day's fishing," suggested the judge, and lifted his newspaper. "Get Mrs. Mitchell to put up some sandwiches for you and make a day of it. Might be a considerable while before you have another chance."

Jonathan stood up, grateful to escape. "That's a good idea, sir. Thanks. I'll see you at dinner."

Jonathan's spirits lifted slightly as he left the lodge and took the path down toward his favorite fishing spot. His thoughts were so tied up with Loyce that when he reached the turn in the path that led away from the trail, he glanced automatically at the flat rock that was a favorite spot of hers. But of course she wasn't there, and his mouth thinned bitterly.

Of course she's not taking any chances on meeting you, you fool, he told himself savagely. She's hiding from you! And that ought to give you a pretty good idea of where you stand with her.

It was late afternoon when he gave up the unsuccessful attempt at fishing and returned to the lodge. He saw none of the family as he went up to his room to clean up for dinner, but when he came downstairs they were all waiting for him and went into the dining room in a small, companionable group.

Loyce, in a crisply fresh cotton dress, sat across the table from Jonathan, her eyes on her plate. Cherry sat opposite her grandfather and chattered gaily as Elsie began serving dinner.

The judge smiled at her flushed, radiant young face and glanced now and then, as dinner progressed, at Loyce's pallor. Beneath the summer's suntan she looked ashen and much older than her years. But it was not until dessert and coffee had been served that the judge made his first move.

He looked up as Elsie placed dessert before him and said, "Ask your mother to come in, will you, Elsie? And Eben, too. This is a family matter, so I felt the whole family should have a part in it."

Elsie looked startled, but disappeared into the kitchen and a moment later returned with Mrs. Mitchell.

"Muv," said the judge, "how long have you and Eben been here at the lodge?"

"Why, ever since you brought the girls here, judge," answered Mrs. Mitchell, obviously puzzled by the question. "That would be eighteen, nineteen years, way I figure it. Elsie was just Cherry's age, and you thought it would be nice for your gals to have somebody to play with."

The judge nodded, while those at the table stared at him in bewilderment.

"And you're not planning to leave, are you Muv?" the judge asked gently.

Mrs. Mitchell stared at him as though she thought he had lost his mind, while Eben stirred restlessly, vaguely alarmed.

"Leave, Judge?" Mrs. Mitchell repeated. "This is our home, judge. Why would we leave?"

The judge nodded, and now his gaze was on Loyce, who was staring at him with wide, shocked eyes.

"Then in case my two granddaughters

222

found husbands for themselves and went away, I wouldn't be alone, would I?" asked the judge, still addressing himself to Mrs. Mitchell, though his eyes were on the swift rush of color that flooded Loyce's face and the startled glance she shot Jonathan.

"Alone? Judge, you'll never be alone as long as one of us Mitchell's has breath in his body," Mrs. Mitchell said sternly.

The judge gave her a warm, grateful smile which vanished as he turned once more to Loyce.

"You see?" he said quietly. "You were going to marry Weldon Hammett and leave the lodge and me. So why can't you marry Jonny and leave with him?"

"I — but then, Cherry and Job weren't engaged," Loyce stammered.

"Look, Judge, I see what you're trying to do," Jonathan began.

"You love her, don't you?" demanded the judge.

"Very much."

"And you want to marry her, don't you?"

"Not like this," said Jonathan, and stood up, thrusting his chair violently backward so that he had to catch it to keep it from falling over. "I don't want an unwilling wife who'll keep looking over her shoulder and feeling guilty because she left you and neglected her duty to you."

"Sit down!" thundered the judge so unexpectedly that they all started and blinked at him. "I'll have order to hold you in contempt of court. I've had all the nonsense about this that I intend to have."

He glared around the table as Jonathan reluctantly seated himself.

"If you think," the judge addressed himself to Loyce, "that I'm going to put up with another year or two of you moping and mewling and whining around because you've lost another love, you, my girl, are sadly mistaken. Either you marry Jonathan and go away with him, or I'll send you down to the

224

'flat-lands' to get a job! And don't think I don't mean that. I intend to have some peace and quiet in my declining years if I have to go and live my myself in a cave."

"But, Gran'sir — " Loyce whimpered.

"Just a second, sir," Jonathan said grimly. "If she has to be forced to marry me, I don't want her."

The judge sighed gustily. "You young people! I often wonder how you can be such utter fools and play fast and loose with all the good things life offers you!"

He looked at Loyce, then at Jonathan and back at Loyce. She was watching him with wide eyes as though she had never seen this somewhat terrifying man before. He was in his old role as a stern judge sitting on the bench, pronouncing judgement on some hapless criminal who stood looking up at him without hope.

"You've had something, my girl, that happens very rarely to anyone," he pointed out: "a second chance at a happy marriage and a good life. Love isn't something like the 'fairy crosses' that the tourists find by the handfuls; it's more like some fine ruby that is found just once, or at most twice in a lifetime. I'm sure you were in love with Hammett; but you were a different girl then. You've grown up a bit — that is, if you'll let yourself."

"I just wanted to look after you the way you've looked after Cherry and me," Loyce stammered miserably.

Mrs. Mitchell sniffed. "A lot of looking after him you've done these last two years, Loyce," she reminded the girl. "Sneaking out of the house before daybreak, taking your lunch with you; sitting at the dinner table a few minutes every evening because he ordered you to; and then sneaking off to your room for dear knows what. A mighty fine companion you've been to him. You've near 'bout worried him to death. Way I see it, he'd be mighty relieved to know you was off somewhere married and happy."

Jonathan stood up, and this time his scowl and tone of his voice told them that he was not staying for further arguments.

"I've never looked on myself as the answer to a maiden's prayer, exactly," he said grimly. "But neither have I thought of myself as a man who had to get a girl's family to force her to marry him. A thing like that could easily give a man an inferiority complex similar to Loyce's. So if you'll excuse me, I have some packing to do."

He turned and strode out of the room, and for a moment after he had gone there was an abashed, uneasy silence behind him. It was the judge who broke it.

"Go after him, girl," he ordered softly.

Loyce shrank, eyes wide, and there were stains of tears on her cheeks.

"Oh, Gran'sir, I can't!" she whispered piteously.

"Because you think it might be humiliating to have to plead with

227

him?" asked her grandfather without mercy.

"Well, of course it would."

"How do you suppose he felt, sitting here listening to us? To me, rather. You didn't have much to say, come to think of it."

"You took me so by surprise, I couldn't think," she replied.

"Well, if you want him you'd better get out there and convince him," the judge reminded her. "If you're worrying about what's going to happen here after you and Cherry are gone, I'll tell you. Eben's son, Ansel, will take over your work and do a mighty fine job of it. Now that's settled. And as for Cherry, she's arranged for Betty Marshall to take over her job. So where is the problem?"

Loyce sat very still for a moment, looking first at her grandfather, then at the Mitchells and last at Cherry, who gave her a tentative but warm smile.

"Looks as if we'd been bounced from our jobs, Loyce. Let's face it and make the best of it," Cherry suggested.

Loyce stood up at last. There was a lovely pink in her cheeks and her eyes were shining as she went out of the room and up the stairs.

Jonathan looked up as she knocked and opened the door. For a long moment he met her eyes and then went back to his packing.

"Jonny, don't go," she whispered faintly.

He apparently did not hear her, and she closed the door and came to stand within arm's reach of him.

"But if you must go, Jonny," she whispered, "take me with you."

For a moment his hands that were stuffing articles into his opened suitcase were still. He did not look up, nor did he speak for a moment. And when he did his voice was curt and sharp. "Sorry! That's out!"

She cringed as though he had struck her, and some of the soft color left her face. But her eyes clung to his, and

229

though her hands clenched tightly she did not give up.

"You said you loved me," she whispered.

"I do. But that doesn't mean I'll settle for any less from you."

"You don't have to, Jonny darling. I love you. Oh, darling, I love you so much." Her voice was shaken, and her hands reached out to him and were drawn swiftly back as he made no effort to accept them.

He straightened, and for a long moment he looked at her coldly. His eyes were bleak, as was his tone when he answered, "Love me so much that your grandfather had to adopt his courtroom manner and sentence you to marry me or get out?"

"He didn't really mean that, Jonny."

"It certainly sounded to me as though he meant exactly what he said," Jonny pointed out grimly. "And who can blame him, after the way you behaved about Hammett? And now when, as he pointed out, you get a second chance at love and you're still afraid!"

"*Afraid?*" she stammered, outraged.

"Afraid!" he repeated as though pounding his point home. "Afraid of leaving your snug little dreary nest here and stepping out somewhere to undertake responsibilities and marriage. And there *are* responsibilities, my girl! Make no mistake about that."

She drew a long, hard breath and admitted her defeat.

For a long moment she met his eyes, and then she said very softly, "I don't blame you for being disgusted with me, for doubting that I love you. I do, but I know now I could never make you believe that. So you'll go away and I'll probably never see you again. But will you kiss me good-bye, darling?"

He stood very still for a moment, his tall body rigid. And then his arms swept out and cradled her close and hard against him, and his cheek was against hers that was tear-wet beneath a lovely rising flush. Their lips found each other and clung. And all confusion

231

and misunderstanding and bitterness was swallowed up in the breathtaking magic kiss . . .

Downstairs in the big living room, Cherry perched on the edge of her chair and watched her grandfather, who was apparently completely absorbed in his book. Suddenly there was a twinkle in Cherry's eyes and she leaned forward, took the book from him, turned it right side up and gave it back to him.

"It's much easier to read if you hold it right side up," she mocked him tenderly.

The judge looked at her sheepishly.

"I suppose it is," he agreed, and looked up toward the stairs. "They've been gone a long time, haven't they?"

"Well, they've got a lot of things to settle," Cherry answered reasonably.

"You *do* think they'll be happy, honey?"

"Well, of course they will," Cherry assured him with such bright confidence that he was relieved. "Jonny's a darling and Loyce is a treasure, and why wouldn't they have themselves a simply super marriage?"

The windows were open to the night. Suddenly she stood up and walked across to one of them and stood leaning there, savoring the sound of the wind through the trees, the faint, faraway barking of a dog, the tinkle of a cow bell from the pasture.

"Listen, Gran'sir," she whispered as though the sound of her voice might destroy the beloved mountain music. "Wind in the pines! Mountain melody! Oh, Gran'sir, I'm so glad I'm marrying a mountain man and can listen to that melody all the rest of my life! It's the most beautiful music in the whole world."

"It is, my dear, it is," he answered gently.

She turned swiftly and came back to drop to her knees beside his chair and to lay her arms across his blanketed, lifeless knees.

"Darling, are you going to miss us just terribly?" she asked softly.

"Scarcely a bit," he answered hardily.

"You're lying, Gran'sir, and I love you for it," she told him. "But don't you worry. I'll be running in every few days, and there'll be vacations when Jonny and Loyce will come down. And we'll bring the children to visit you."

"Well, you'd better," said the judge, and his smile was warm and tender for all that he tried to make his voice stern, "or I'll get out an injunction against you. Could you just possibly name the first boy Bramblett? Or would Job mind?"

"Phooey for Job! The second one can be named Job, junior." Cherry laughed and drew herself up so that she could put her arms about him and hold him close. "Bramblett would be a lovely name! Gavin Bramblett Tallent! I think he'll like that! And then there'll always be a Bramblett at the lodge. And that's as it should be!"

Upstairs a door opened, and there

were footsteps in the hall and on the stairs. Cherry stood up with a lovely, graceful movement, her hand still on the judge's shoulder as she watched them come slowly down the stairs. One look at their faces, even without Jonathan's arm about Loyce, told her that all was well with these two, and her heart swelled until she was breathless with its warm sweetness.

The beloved mountain melody that she had always loved had become a love song, and nothing nicer could ever have happened at Crossways Lodge, she told herself joyously as she went forward to offer her congratulations and her heartfelt good wishes.

"He's forgiven me, Gran'sir," Loyce said radiantly.

"I had the feeling he would," the judge answered, his eyes twinkling. "Congratulations, my boy. I know you'll both be very happy. Now maybe you'd like to forgive me for playing Cupid with a baseball bat. It *was* pretty rough, I admit."

Jonathan laughed as he wrung the judge's hand, keeping his arm about Loyce.

"Rough it was, Your Honor," he agreed, "but effective. It made us both realize some important things we might otherwise have overlooked."

"Fine! That's good to hear. A judge likes to know his pronouncements are effective." He looked up at Loyce. "Do you forgive me, honey, for the scene I made at the table?"

"Of course, darling. How could I not? I deserved every bit of it, and if you hadn't been so brutally frank, Jonny might have got away from me."

She was wide-eyed with shock at the thought, and Jonathan laughed and drew her close.

"I'd have come back," he promised her softly.

"Promise you always will?" she pleaded.

"I can't, darling. I don't expect ever to go away from you so that I can come back. You and I are a team, honey. 'Whither thou goest, I will go' — remember?"

Cherry watched them with a mist of happy tears in her eyes as they turned and went across the living room and out to the verandah. For she knew that the beloved mountain music that meant so much to her would now be ringing in their hearts, and it would be a love song neither would ever forget.

THE END

Other titles in the Linford Romance Library:

A YOUNG MAN'S FANCY
Nancy Bell

Six people get together for reasons of their own, and the result is one of misunderstanding, suspicion and mounting tension.

THE WISDOM OF LOVE
Janey Blair

Barbie meets Louis and receives flattering proposals, but her reawakened affection for Jonah develops into an overwhelming passion.

MIRAGE IN THE MOONLIGHT
Mandy Brown

En route to an island to be secretary to a multi-millionaire, Heather's stubborn loyalty to her former flatmate plunges her into a grim hazard.

A DANGEROUS MAN
Anne Goring

Photographer Polly Burton was on safari in Mombasa when she met enigmatic Leon Hammond. But unpredictability was the name of the game where Leon was concerned.

PRECIOUS INHERITANCE
Joan Moules

Karen's new life working for an authoress took her from Sussex to a foreign airstrip and a kidnapping; to a real life adventure as gripping as any in the books she typed.

VISION OF LOVE
Grace Richmond

When Kathy takes over the rundown country kennels she finds Alec Stinton, a local vet, very helpful. But their friendship arouses bitter jealousy and a tragedy seems inevitable.

HOSPITAL BY THE LAKE
Anne Durham

Nurse Marguerite Ingleby was always ready to become personally involved with her patients, to the despair of Brian Field, the Senior Surgical Registrar, who loved her.

VALLEY OF CONFLICT
David Farrell

Isolated in a hostel in the French Alps, Ann Russell sees her fiancé being seduced by a young girl. Then comes the avalanche that imperils their lives.

NURSE'S CHOICE
Peggy Gaddis

A proposal of marriage from the incredibly handsome and wealthy Reagan was enough to upset any girl — and Brooke Martin was no exception.

HEAVEN IS HIGH
Anne Hampson

The new heir to the Manor of Marbeck had been found. But it was rather unfortunate that when he arrived unexpectedly he found an uninvited guest, complete with stetson and high boots.

LOVE WILL COME
Sarah Devon

June Baker's boss was not really her idea of her ideal man, but when she went from third typist to boss's secretary overnight she began to change her mind.

ESCAPE TO ROMANCE
Kay Winchester

Oliver and Jean first met on Swale Island. They were both trying to begin their lives afresh, but neither had bargained for complications from the past.

THE WAYWARD HEART
Eileen Barry

Disaster-prone Katherine's nickname was "Kate Calamity", but her boss went too far with an outrageous proposal, which because of her latest disaster, she could not refuse.

FOUR WEEKS IN WINTER
Jane Donnelly

Tessa wasn't looking forward to meeting Paul Mellor again — she had made a fool of herself over him once before. But was Orme Jared's solution to her problem likely to be the right one?

SURGERY BY THE SEA
Sheila Douglas

Medical student Meg hadn't really wanted to go and work with a G.P. on the Welsh coast although the job had its compensations. But Owen Roberts was certainly not one of them!

ROMANTIC LEGACY
Cora Mayne

As kennelmaid to the Armstrongs, Ann Brown, had no idea that she would become the central figure in a web of mystery and intrigue.

THE RELENTLESS TIDE
Jill Murray

Steve Palmer shared Nurse Marie Blane's love of the sea and small boats. Marie's other passion was her step-brother. But when danger threatened who should she turn to — her step-brother or the man who stirred emotions in her heart?

ROMANCE IN NORWAY
Cora Mayne

Nancy Crawford hopes that her visit to Norway will help her to start life again. She certainly finds many surprises there, including unexpected happiness.

WITH SOMEBODY ELSE
Theresa Charles

Rosamond sets off for Cornwall with Hugo to meet his family, blissfully unaware of the shocks in store for her.

A SUMMER FOR STRANGERS
Claire Hamilton

Because she had lost her job, her flat and she had no money, Tabitha agreed to pose as Adam's future wife although she believed the scheme to be deceitful and cruel.

VILLA OF SINGING WATER
Angela Petron

The disquieting incidents that occurred at the Vatican and the Colosseum did not trouble Jan at first, but then they became increasingly unpleasant and alarming.

CRUSADING NURSE
Jane Converse

It was handsome Dr. Corbett who opened Nurse Susan Leighton's eyes and who set her off on a lonely crusade against some powerful enemies and a shattering struggle against the man she loved.

WILD ENCHANTMENT
Christina Green

Rowan's agreeable new boss had a dream of creating a famous perfume using her precious Silverstar, but Rowan's plans were very different.

DESERT ROMANCE
Irene Ord

Sally agrees to take her sister Pam's place as La Chartreuse the dancer, but she finds out there is more to it than dyeing her hair red and looking like her sister.

HEART OF ICE
Marie Sidney

How was January to know that not only would the warmth of the Swiss people thaw out her frozen heart, but that she too would play her part in helping someone to live again?

LUCKY IN LOVE
Margaret Wood

Companion-secretary to wealthy gambler Laura Duxford, who lived in Monaco, seemed to Melanie a fabulous job. Especially as Melanie had already lost her heart to Laura's son, Julian.

NURSE TO PRINCESS JASMINE
Lilian Woodward

Nick's surgeon brother, Tom, performs an operation on an Arabian princess, and she invites Tom, Nick and his fiancé to Omander, where a web of deceit and intrigue closes about them.

CASTLE IN THE SUN
Cora Mayne

Emma's invalid sister, Kym, needed a warm climate, and Emma jumped at the chance of a job on a Mediterranean island. But Emma soon finds that intrigues and hazards lurk on the sunlit isle.

BEWARE OF LOVE
Kay Winchester

Carol Brampton resumes her nursing career when her family is killed in a car accident. With Dr. Patrick Farrell she begins to pick up the pieces of her life, but is bitterly hurt when insinuations are made about her to Patrick.

DARLING REBEL
Sarah Devon

When Jason Farradale's secretary met with an accident, her glamorous stand-in was quite unable to deal with one problem in particular.

THE PRICE OF PARADISE
Jane Arbor

It was a shock to Fern to meet her estranged husband on an island in the middle of the Indian Ocean, but to discover that her father had engineered it puzzled Fern. What did he hope to achieve?

DOCTOR IN PLASTER
Lisa Cooper

When Dr. Scott Sutcliffe is injured, Nurse Caroline Hurst has to cope with a very demanding private case. But when she realises her exasperating patient has stolen her heart, how can Caroline possibly stay?

A TOUCH OF HONEY
Lucy Gillen

Before she took the job as secretary to author Robert Dean, Cadie had heard how charming he was, but that wasn't her first impression at all.

ENCORE
Helga Moray

Craig and Janet realise that their true happiness lies with each other, but it is only under traumatic circumstances that they can be reunited.

NICOLETTE
Ivy Preston

When Grant Alston came back into her life, Nicolette was faced with a dilemma. Should she follow the path of duty or the path of love?

THE GOLDEN PUMA
Margaret Way

Catherine's time was spent looking after her father's Queensland farm. But what life was there without David, who wasn't interested in her?

1		25		49		73	2/13		
2	10/10	26		50	1/14	74			
3		27		51		75			
4	11/04	28		52	3/10	76			
5		29		53		77	8/32/19		
6	12/5	30	8/15	54		78			
7		31		55		79	9/07		
8		32		56		80			
9	1/19	33		57		81			
10		34		58	2/08	82	2/09		
11		35		59		83			
12	9.12	36		60		84			
13	7/14	37		61	7/18	85			
14		38		62		86			
15		39		63		87			
16	3/18	40		64		88			
17		41		65		89			
18		42		66		90			
19		43		67		91			
20		44		68		92			
21		45		69		COMMUNITY SERVICES			
22		46		70					
23		47		71		NPT/111			
24		48		72